GOLD
RUSH
GIRL

Gold Rush Girl

Avi

CANDLEWICK PRESS

Copyright © 2020 by Avi Wortis Inc.

First edition 2020

Library of Congress Catalog Card Number pending
ISBN 978-1-5362-0679-1

19 20 21 22 23 24 LBM 10 9 8 7 6 5 4 3 2 1

Printed in Melrose Park, IL, U.S.A.

This book was typeset in Adobe Caslon Pro.

Candlewick Press
99 Dover Street
Somerville, Massachusetts 02144

visit us at www.candlewick.com

For Isabella and Zeke

· I ·

HAVE YOU EVER BEEN STRUCK BY LIGHTNING?
I have.

I write not of the sparkling that bolts from the sky, but of *gold*, the yellow metal buried in the earth and the shatter-wit world of those who seek it. That world turned me topsy-turvy, so that I did things I never dreamed I would or could do.

It began, fittingly, in a leap year: 1848. I was thirteen years old.

My family — Father (Randolph Blaisdell); Mother (Abigail Pell Blaisdell); my younger brother, Jacob; and I, Victoria, most often called Tory — was residing in the small-est state in these United States: Rhode Island. We had a home in Providence, the state's major city, with its fine buildings, wealth, tranquility, and a population of forty thousand.

Our home was 15 Sheldon Street, a modest but agreeable wooden house on the east side of town. It stood upon "The Hill," as it was smartly called, above commercial Wickenden Street. We had a cook and one servant, both of whom lived in our attic.

Our lives were comfortable, with nothing unusual *ever* happening. Indeed, my early family life was untroubled, as smooth as Chinese silk. I questioned nothing, not about the world or about myself. My entire universe was Sheldon Street, which meant I knew everyone as they knew me. As for my social life, it consisted of calling and receiving among a small group of proper neighborhood girls.

As one grows up, it can take a while to understand that sometimes it is *not* your mother or father who have the greatest influence on your life. Thus it was but gradually that I came to realize that the person who shaped my life more than any other was my mother's older sister, Aunt Lavinia.

Since the two sisters were from the distinguished Rhode Island Pell family, Lavinia already considered herself quite the queen. Then, before I was born, she married Quincy Fellows, a wealthy Pawtucket cloth-factory owner. That made her—in her mind—an *empress*.

A tall, big woman, with hanging coils of braid alongside her puffy face, which peered out from a deep, dark bonnet, she wore long, wide gowns with bulging sleeves, a shape that made me think of her as a walking mountain, and a volcano at that. Indeed, she constantly erupted with lava-like judgments, advice, and instructions as to how my family should live our lives. All of which is to say, while my mother and father raised me, their words were almost always prefaced by "As your aunt Lavinia suggests . . ."

One of Aunt Lavinia's judgments—which I was shocked to discover—was that my mother had *lowered* her station in life by marrying my father.

Father was a man of middle age and modest height. Quite portly, he had a round, smooth, shaved face and fair hair brushed with care. His soft pink hands—somewhat ink stained—were what you would expect of someone who wielded pen, not pickax. At home or at work, he attired himself in common gentleman's fashion—English frock coat, vest, knotted neck cloth, tan pants, and tall black silk hat.

He worked as an accountant for Pratt and Willinghast, a respectable trading business, which had its offices on Peck Street in the middle of Providence. Significantly, it was a position secured for him by Aunt Lavinia's husband, a fact which she did not let Father (or Mother) forget.

Still, after ten years of service, Father received a silver pocket watch in recognition of his good work. He liked to bring it out at regular intervals so as to suggest that he was a busy man. In fact, I came to understand it was displayed mostly to show Aunt Lavinia that he was worthy. But then, as I came to realize, Father's highest ambition was to become acceptable to Aunt Lavinia, and he chose to do so by agreeing to all her advice and judgments.

As for my mother, she had a kindhearted, loving nature and looked after us all, trying her best to shield us from her sister's dictates. By way of personal occupation, other than supervising her children's upbringing and managing the household, she had her reading (popular romances such as *The Betrothed*) and needlework to do. Yet while Mother was a quiet soul, sometimes, when I watched her sewing, it seemed as if she were frustrated with her life and used her needle to pierce the fabric of her world.

Exasperated by my parents' constant deference to Aunt Lavinia, it was upon my younger brother, Jacob, that I bestowed my deepest affections. More than anyone else, he was willing to listen to my endless prattle. Most of all, he didn't criticize me. We were as close as kin can be, and I enjoyed his company greatly.

Jacob—four years younger than I—had a pleasing, apple-cheeked sweetness. An earnest, serious, almost solemn boy, he was not given to mischief. When he played with his school friends, he did so quietly, without much zest.

He was fond of music and enjoyed whistling the popular songs of the day. That said, his whistling told me that he was troubled. Whereas Jacob considered me hot-brained, he fretted far too much, and worry made him agitated.

Jacob appeared to be the least bothered by how much our lives were governed by my aunt. But then it was Jacob of whom Aunt Lavinia most approved. She, who had no children of her own, once said, "Jacob is a perfect child. He is quiet and does what he is told. We should all encourage Victoria to be more like her brother."

Once she informed me, "You should know, Victoria, that someday Jacob will be the head of the family and you will need to defer to him."

Young though I was, I was much distressed and replied, "Jacob shall have his life. I shall have mine."

To which Aunt Lavinia scolded, "Nonsense. A girl's life should be solely dedicated to taking care of others."

I'm sure that made me pout-mouthed.

Because I resisted my aunt's dictates, she was particularly harsh on me, finding me too independent, too bold, and far too free with my opinions. But the truth is, there were few aspects of my life which did not come under her firm declarations.

"Victoria should dress this way." That meant, for example, that I must never go outside without gloves and bonnet.

"Victoria should have proper acquaintances." This meant that the Misses Biggs were *not* suitable friends whereas the Misses Colchester *were*. I was never told the reasons.

"Victoria should be taking dancing lessons from Mrs. Coldbrett's Academy of Dancery."

I attended weekly.

And: "To call Victoria *Tory* is vulgar."

Once — I was no more than ten — she told me, "Unless you change your opinionated ways, you will not find a suitable man willing to marry you."

My retort was "I intend to remain self-governing."

When Jacob turned six (I was ten), he began to attend a school selected by my aunt: the Rhode Island Institute of Instruction, in Providence. She further proclaimed that it was sufficient for a girl to be educated at home, save Sunday church school. My parents did as she advised. I did *not* go to school.

Whereas Jacob went to school tamely, I objected to *not* going and did so strongly. Why, I argued, should I not get an education? Was I not the eldest child? Was I not quick-witted and eager?

Father consulted his pocket watch and said, "We shall do what Aunt Lavinia advises."

While I did not go to school, my mother sympathized with me. She took it upon herself to teach me to read and write (as, she told me, her mother had taught her).

Additionally, I secretly persuaded Jacob to share all his school lessons with me. That allowed me to be educated on my own — furtively. The truth is, I far surpassed him.

I was therefore soon reading a great deal. Alas, the books in our home were too few, too limited. Having a desire for more knowledge, I took such small monies as I had saved (birthday and Christmas gifts) and, telling no one, walked downhill to the Providence Athenaeum, the city's fine library. But when I placed my sparse coins on the counter and informed the white-haired gentleman secretary that I wished to purchase a membership, he told me I had not nearly enough.

Disappointment must have clouded my face.

The secretary considered me with a kindly smile, paused a long moment, and then leaned down and whispered, "Since you are so young and eager, I shall give you a free subscription. But," he added, finger to his lips, "you must not tell anyone."

I went from rejection to rapture.

I borrowed books and hid them in my private room. At night, while the whole house slept, I read voraciously by candlelight and learned that stealthy reading is absolutely sublime. Reading became my other world. I discovered and consumed volumes by Mr. Poe, Mr. Dickens, and Miss Austen. Did I understand them all? Of course not. But then people do not generally grasp the true value of reading: It is not to learn about *others*. It is to learn about oneself.

Thus it was that I came upon the recently published auto-biography of *Jane Eyre*. That book transformed my life.

·2·

I ADORED *JANE EYRE*, THE PERSON AND THE BOOK. In that book—it was as if I were reading a mirror—I read about Jane Eyre's aunt, the tyrannical Mrs. Reed, who, I had no doubt, was much like my aunt Lavinia.

More than that: I revered the narration for its wisdom, ardent emotions, and beyond all else, the heroine's fierce independence. How Jane suffered. How cruelly she was treated. How much she overcame. How splendid were her impulsive emotions. Her bravery. Her courage. Wisdom. Her great love. Oh, how I yearned to live just such a life, full of trial, rebellion, and adventure.

(Only much later would I learn that the book was a work of fiction. When I first encountered it, I truly believed it to be the memoir of a real person and was thus enthralled the more. Since then, I have come to regard fiction as fact without dates.)

Most important, it was in *Jane Eyre* (chapter 23) that I found this extraordinary sentence:

Your will shall decide your destiny.

Those words became my guiding light, my ideal. Oh, how I wished my will could decide *my* destiny.

The more books I read, the more convinced I became that I must become up-to-date in all my thoughts and live a life of independent and heightened sentiments. I began to appreciate that the smartest thing I could do was to acknowledge how ignorant I was. I saw old Providence as far too passive, with nothing spirited or fresh. I yearned to be free of Aunt Lavinia's rules. How grand, I thought, to be caught up in mystery, strong feelings, and adventure (like Jane Eyre), to live a life written with exclamation points!!!!

Increasingly resistant to my aunt's opinions and rules, I came to think of her not merely as a controlling force but as a bully.

When I turned thirteen, I looked up the word *teen* and was much pleased to discover the early meaning of the term was "angry, vexed," and "enraged." Thus, being, as it were, licensed by my dictionary, I chose to become fully *teen,* which to me meant that I had to move beyond Sheldon Street.

How can I best express this?

Since Rhode Island is a seagoing place, the state's symbol is an anchor. However, in Latin, an anchor—*ancora*—is a symbol of hope. Thus the state's motto is *Hope.* Observe the jest. An *anchor* is something that keeps you in place, whereas *ancora/hope* suggests change.

As you can see, I began to desire not Rhode Island's *anchor,* which held me in place, but Rhode Island's *ancora,* which meant *hope.* My desire was to be free of Aunt Lavinia's directives.

I began modestly. One day I informed my brother that I was going to walk downtown to the Arcade to buy a ribbon.

"Alone?" he said. "Across the river?"

I said, "Alone. Across the river."

"Without a chaperone?"

"Without a chaperone."

"What," he said, "would Aunt Lavinia say?"

Jacob's words stiffened my resolve. I said, "I don't care what she says. But you mustn't tell."

As I left the house, I could hear Jacob whistling.

I walked down the hill, then across the Providence River to the city center, a distance of more than a mile. I had never walked alone so far from home.

Despite my resolution and my desire for rebellion, I was quite nervous and walked with care, acutely aware that I was an unchaperoned girl, rare for someone of my station. Also, everyone was a stranger, and these strangers mostly men.

Feeling that every male eye was upon me—and those eyes malevolent—I kept my gloved hands clasped and my eyes straight forward, pretending not to notice anyone.

I managed to find a shop, quickly purchased a yard of blue ribbon, and went straight back home, altogether thankful when I reached it. Upon my return, such was Jacob's relief that he hugged me.

"You were gone so long, I almost went to save you," he confessed.

I did not tell him of my own unease, or my sense of triumph. Yes, that dictionary of mine told me there were many synonyms for *freedom. Liberty. Self-determination. Autonomy.* But as far as I was concerned, the most exciting meaning was *boldness.*

Perhaps the best illustration of my life at that time was my weekly dancing lessons.

As I have set down, Aunt Lavinia had insisted I attend lessons at Mrs. Coldbrett's Academy of Dancery. There I was expected to learn to dance while absorbing proper social etiquette, which is to say, how to conduct my social life.

The classes were instructed by a Mrs. Coldbrett, who

always reminded me of a giraffe (I had seen a picture of one in a book) in a long black dress. She used an ebony cane to beat the time while crooked-backed, speechless Mr. Coldbrett plucked the piano keys.

The quadrille, the grand march, and the waltz were taught. The polka — of which I had only heard — was considered unrefined and was *not* taught.

Though young, we girls were always dressed in good fashion. White gloves for all, high-necked, long muslin dresses of checked design with three-tiered sleeves. Boys came in cutaway jackets, black cravats, and narrow trousers. Some even wore top hats.

Of course, we had dance cards, which listed, by number, one's partner for each dance. They were filled out by Mrs. Coldbrett, who was most careful to make *proper* matches.

(Note: I was told to bring these cards home so that Aunt Lavinia might inspect and evaluate my dance partners.)

The byword at the dancing school was *serenity*, with no displays of emotion. I can well recall Mrs. Coldbrett reminding us that:

> "Attention should be particularly paid to giving the hands in a proper manner, to the avoiding of affectation in doing so, to keeping the united hands at a height suited to both parties, shunning the slightest

grasping or weighing upon the hands of another, to avoid twisting your partner."

The lessons were followed by a formal tea, during which we were required to make polite conversation. Needless to say, we girls were *never* to initiate a conversation. Mrs. Coldbrett had directives about conversations too, such as:

> "Don't talk in a high, shrill voice, and avoid nasal tones. Cultivate a chest voice; learn to moderate your tones. Talk always in a low register, but not too low. Avoid any air of mystery when speaking to those next to you; it is ill bred and in excessively bad taste."

Aunt Lavinia thoroughly approved of such ideas. For my part, I desired nothing more than to acquire that "air of mystery."

One day in the winter of 1848, I was attending my dance lesson. Having danced, it was teatime, with delicate china cups, and we girls and boys were chatting in the required way.

"Miss Victoria, how pleasant to see you. How are you this day?" This was asked of me by a snub-nosed, big-eared, twelve-year-old boy named Archibald Ackroyd, who was a head shorter than me.

"Most fine, sir. Thank you."

"Have you had an agreeable week?"

"Most certainly. And may I inquire about you, Master Ackroyd?"

Though I spoke so, I was feeling most disconnected, bored, barely listening to the mindless chatter of the children around me. I suspect my indifference was because the night before I had been reading Mary Shelley's *Frankenstein*, wherein are such glorious such passages as:

> "To me the walls of a dungeon or a palace were alike hateful. The cup of life was poisoned forever, and although the sun shone upon me, as upon the happy and gay of heart, I saw around me nothing but a dense and frightful darkness."

You can understand, then, how struck I was by the nothingness of the youth surrounding me, how thoroughly empty of vigorous ideas, how void of real emotions, how complacent, how potato-headed these *suitable* children all were.

That evening, with great indignation, I shared such thoughts with Jacob. To my frustration, my brother was puzzled by my reaction to that dance lesson. Of course, he had not read *Frankenstein*. In truth, if I had told him it had been written by a nineteen-year-old *girl* he would have been horrified—not so much by the monster but by the girl.

"You had better," he warned, "not tell Aunt Lavinia what you read."

I informed Mother I would *not* go to dancing classes again. Among my grievances: "Why must I always do and think as your sister says?"

"She is wealthy, older, and wiser."

I replied, "She opposed your marriage to Father."

Mother assured me that her marriage had been a love match. Then she smiled, patted my hand, and said, "All too soon you will grow up, and *then* you will understand the ways of a girl in the world. Be patient, Tory."

As far as I was concerned, *patience* was merely the *pretense* of good-mannered waiting—another anchor—when, in fact, one is actually in a hurry. More and more I wanted a change. Alas, I had come to realize that the more contented a family *appears*, the more often the parents fail to notice when the eldest child changes.

But as it happened, I did not have to wait long for enormous shifts to happen. That was because something unforeseen occurred, something that transformed our placid lives.

Father lost his position—and all his wages.

·3·

FATHER'S PLACE OF EMPLOYMENT, PRATT AND Willinghast—which did a great deal of trade with France—went bankrupt. This unexpected and catastrophic event was the result of the violent revolution that occurred in that distant European country. When Father lost his position, he lost his entire income, which is to say, our whole means of living.

Let me be fair: it was not just Father who experienced unemployment. Rhode Island—a commercial, manufacturing, and international shipping port—suffered an economic panic. *Many* professional and wage-earning men were unable to find work.

My father's predicament distressed him greatly. "I have failed my family," he told us, while clutching his pocket watch as if to display the evidence that he *had* been of value.

Then, fairly groaning, he added, "Aunt Lavinia must not know."

"I don't intend to tell her," agreed Mother. And she gave Jacob and me a severe look, which told us not to say anything either.

As the days passed, Father kept insisting, "I shall find something," but in fact, he did not. It was as if a failure in one part of his life spread to all. His lack of gainful employment shamed him into total inaction. As his joblessness continued, he sank into a deep, despondent melancholy and did little more than sit in the parlor, licking his thumb so as to go through the newspaper.

One night, wanting to encourage him, I felt best to remind him of something I learned in Sunday school. Citing Proverbs 13:4, I said, "The soul of the sluggard desireth and hath nothing: but the soul of the diligent shall be made fat."

"You sound like Aunt Lavinia."

I was horrified. Was I, against all desire, all hope, becoming like her? No. I studied that proverb and decided it was much like the brave words in *Jane Eyre*: *Your will shall decide your destiny.*

That said, we hardly knew what would happen to us. Father's spirits, already low, sank lower. As you might guess, his situation caused tension at home. I believe it was that which caused Mother to become ill. Endlessly fatigued, she had severe headaches and constant feelings of stress. Dear old Dr. Laxton said she was suffering from an illness I could hardly say: neurasthenia. He insisted she rest in bed.

With funds dwindling, we dismissed the servant. Let go the cook. Unable to pay the fees, Jacob stopped going to school. Since Mother was infirm, I — who did not believe in false pride — cooked and cleaned.

Nonetheless there soon came a time when our funds were so depleted that Aunt Lavinia had to be informed.

How did she respond?

"It must have been your husband's fault," she told Mother. All the same, she provided some monies that we might live. That made things worse. Now there was *nothing* she did not oversee. One of her orders: "Victoria must take care of Jacob."

Thus it was that Jacob came under my exclusive care. I fed him, laid out his daily clothing, solved whatever problems he encountered, heard his woes, his worries, and tried to smooth the wrinkles in his life.

This was truly a change of living for me, but not the one I desired. I confess I found my life increasingly yawny. To choose your younger brother's day-to-day clothing, to stir his pudding, is *not* stimulating. As for living under the restrictive tyranny of my aunt, that was insufferable. Oh, how more than ever did

I desire greater change, something that would truly alter *my* entire life.

Having decided I would *not* be like my father, and do *nothing*, or give way to weakness like Mother on her sofa, I extended my life outside Sheldon Street. That is, I took the rash and unusual step—for one of my condition and age—of securing a position in a dressmaker's shop—the proprietress being an acquaintance of Mother's. I did so on my own. This employment—sewing dresses—let me earn ten cents an hour. I told Jacob that when I was working, he would have to take care of himself. He was not pleased.

Need I say it? We kept my employment a secret from Aunt Lavinia.

Aside from the close work of sewing, I was given the task of arranging bolts of cloth. To my shock, they were quite heavy. At first I despaired that I could ever do the work. But determined to shrink from *nothing*, I found myself equal to the lifting task. I actually became stronger.

Was I happy doing this? Of course not. But had not, I reminded myself, Jane Eyre been confronted with a cruel fate—orphaned, ill-treated by *her* aunt, abused at boarding school—only to rise high above it all? I chose to take my circumstance as a test of my will.

While Father did not object to my working, his pride was

such that he refused my earnings. I, therefore, saved my money and imagined solving our family crisis by someday saying, "Here. I have labored hard. Take the money I have earned and hoarded. We shall not starve."

I constantly practiced that speech.

But before I could give it, our lives changed once again.

It was late November of 1848 when reports began to swirl through Providence that *gold* had been discovered in the West, in California. (California is the immense territory which had just been annexed by the United States after our recent war with Mexico.) The rumors insisted that this California gold could be acquired by merely bending over and plucking nuggets from the ground.

As you might imagine, this prospect brought considerable excitement to Rhode Island, an economically distressed community. As a result, many an unemployed man decided to rush west. The sudden furor exemplified the saying, "Wealth inspires many, but *easy* wealth inspires multitudes."

When these reports of California gold first began to circulate, Father dismissed them as no more than wild-goose gabble. "Such fabulous stories cannot be true," he insisted.

Not long after, however — it was in early December of 1848 — Father gathered us round Mother's sofa. With barely suppressed excitement, he read aloud from the Providence *Journal* what the president of the United States, the Honorable

James Polk, had stated to the United States Congress about California:

> "The accounts of the abundance of gold in that terri-
> tory are of such an extraordinary character as would
> scarcely command belief were they not corroborated
> by the authentic reports of officers in the public
> service."

Father put down the paper, looked around at his mysti-
fied family with a face flushed with excitement, and said,
"Did you hear those words? 'Gold of such an extraordinary
character.'

"The president," my father stressed, "would *not* lie.

"It seems to me," he went on with more life than I had
seen from him in weeks, "that since I cannot solve our finan-
cial problems here, I should go to California, where I can
gather my share of this *abundant* gold. As soon as I do, all our
problems will be solved. It will also show Aunt Lavinia the
kind of man I am."

How like Father, the ever-careful man. It took someone
of the highest authority — the president of the United States,
higher even than Aunt Lavinia — to give him, as it were,
permission to radically change his situation.

I had once seen a footrace at Jacob's school in which a man

began the contest by shooting off a pistol. Father's decision to go west was a pistol shot for me. When I heard Father's unexpected words, my heart thrilled. Here was adventure and excitement delivered directly into the bosom of my family. Here was a way I could escape Aunt Lavinia. Which is to say, from the moment I heard Father's words, I discovered my destiny: I too *must* go to California.

·4·

T HAT FATHER WOULD BECOME A FORTUNE HUNTER
is something I would never have predicted. His habits
had been altogether regular, his attitudes predictable, and his
conversations, dare I say, were, to me, like lump-filled oatmeal.
Not a soupçon of enchanting ideas. Or action. Caution was the
fabric from which his soul had been fashioned.

An example:

Like many in Rhode Island, Father believed in slavery's
abolition. So in the fall of 1848, he attended the Anti-Slavery
Conference held in Providence. I begged to go along but was
refused permission. But after he had gone, I slipped out of our
house (dressed as much as a lady as I could), walked into town,
and mingled midst the crowd at the back of the auditorium.

Oh, the terrible tales I heard about the suffering of black people. It made me ill. I also learned about an organization called the Anti-Slavery Convention of American Women.

That night I announced that I wished to join this women's group immediately and *do* something about the scourge of slavery. Not only did my father absolutely forbid me from doing so, but I was also severely scolded for even attending the meeting.

"All very well for you to have noble *thoughts*," he lectured me. "But young ladies are meant to stay home, not fix the world. What would your aunt say?"

Burning with righteous anger, I replied, "You, sir, though you attended the convention, are *doing* nothing to rid the world of this evil." Then I turned my back and walked away.

Not long after that scolding came Father's astonishing announcement about going to California. It was as if he, hitherto a man glued to the earth, was prepared to travel to the moon.

"I don't intend to change our lives *completely*," he informed his astonished family. "Once I go and collect some of the gold from the *extraordinary* abundance, we shall simply relocate ourselves in California. Have no doubt; business establishments with the growing Pacific trade will need double-entry bookkeeping. We shall return to our regular life. The only thing that will change is our geography. But if I'm to regain our fortunes, I must hurry. Many are already going." There was no debate. Father *was* going to California.

From that day forward, Father's only interest, concern, talk, objective was *gold*. He was caught up in what, along the East Coast, was soon known as gold fever.

But I saw it for what it was: Father wished to go to California because he thought finding wealth would be *easy*. That wealth, he thought, would enable him to take up a position *exactly* as he had at Pratt and Willinghast. He was not so much seeking the *future* as he was trying to regain his past.

Even so, when my mother's sister heard of Father's plan, she was strongly opposed. "This is unthinkable. Utter folly. It must not happen."

If I'd had any doubts, her words convinced me that it *should* happen. I did everything to encourage Father's decision, praising him for his courage and his wisdom.

As for Mother, though she was at first much taken aback by Father's decision, she soon became accepting and supportive. Perhaps, she told me, California *would* solve all our problems. Upon that expectation, her health improved somewhat. It was only then that I began to grasp that she too resented her sister's interference and control of our lives. I loved her more for that.

Jacob, who had become bored with not going to school, was swept along by Father's venture. Father's new great wealth, he informed me, would allow us a new house — most likely better than our Sheldon Street home, and with more servants. It would also put him in the best school, with proper friends.

He therefore pleaded that he be allowed to go west and share in what he deemed a grand adventure. Father said he could go.

I trust you have noticed that in all this hubbub there was no mention of *me*.

I have thought hard about families, and I think they are rather like the United States. That is, there is but one union, but each state is different and each has its own government. As far as I was concerned, I was my own state. My own government. For make no mistake, I saw Father's decision as a way to remove myself from the anchor that was Rhode Island, and thereby embrace *ancora*—hope.

I began by announcing that "I believe I too should go to California."

To my delight, Jacob agreed with me. True, I quickly realized it was only because he fancied the notion that once we were there, I would take care of him.

To that, I groaned but took care to do so only *inwardly*.

Mother, more reasoned, told Father that there was nothing I could do for her which a servant could not accomplish.

"But once you," she reminded Father, "are at the gold mines and have found a comfortable home—which I assume you'll do quickly—you'll need someone to keep it clean and in order. As a girl, Tory is best suited for that. She'll be much more helpful to you there than being here with me."

I was not pleased by those *domestic* prospects, but once again decided silence should be the preferred disguise and therefore kept my thoughts to myself lest I be left behind.

Alas, even then, Father's response was "Is not Tory's greater obligation as a young woman to stay and care for her ill mother? I am sure Aunt Lavinia would say as much."

As you might guess, *that* was reason (however *un*reasonable) enough to pitch my desire to go west even higher.

"Besides," continued Father, "as your aunt has said, a girl is too frail to undertake such an arduous expedition."

I—who had spent days sewing and lifting heavy bolts of cloth—was mortified.

Please, do not misunderstand: I love my father, but he is one of those men who rarely change their ideas. Then, when he *does* alter his views, he claims he has *always* held such thoughts and hews to the new ones as rigidly as the old. It was apparent to me that these new ideas were designed to get only what *he* wanted.

Thus it was decreed I *must* stay with Mother in Providence. The two of us would join Father in California *after* he gained his fortune.

Ah! But recall my motto: *My will shall decide my destiny.* I had already decided that California was my destiny.

Not allowed to go? I reminded myself that, just as for Jane Eyre, each new problem was but a riddle-me-ree to be solved. I would have to act for myself. I, therefore, waited for my opportunity.

Meanwhile, for Father, the first great question was, How might he travel west?

It appeared there were those who actually walked across the entire continent by way of the Great Western Desert. It was the cheapest way, but surely the most strenuous.

Or he might take a ship to Panama, and then find a way to traverse the isthmus and thence (again by ship) to California. That route held the grave danger of jungle illness.

Or he could sail around the Horn of South America. That journey covered fourteen *thousand* miles and took as long as *seven* months. Nonetheless, while it was the longest journey— in time and space—it was considered safest. Also, Father could take a direct passage from Providence, which was a major sea-port at the head of Narragansett Bay. The bay, in turn, led to the Atlantic Ocean.

Father, ever the prudent man, chose to sail from Providence and go around the Horn.

The next question was that of cost. The newspaper was full of advertisements for passenger tickets to the West Coast that cost at a minimum two hundred and fifty dollars. Of course, once in California, he must have other expenses: the right clothing, mining tools, and housing. At the moment, our family funds were exceedingly low. To raise enough money for his trip, he decided to sell our Sheldon Street home, his only source of ready cash.

"Since we shall all resettle in California," he informed us, "we'll have no need for this house. I shall sell it and use the money to carry us west."

Sell our house! Hurrah for being *plucky*. How exciting all these alterations.

Alas, Mother's health did not yet allow her to leave her sofa and travel. Dr. Laxton's word was law. Only when he deemed her fully recovered might she voyage out.

"Women are by nature weak," the doctor proclaimed with all the gravity of his Harvard Medical School degree. Clearly, he had not read *Jane Eyre*.

Therefore, it was agreed that Mother should stay in Aunt Lavinia's house until such time as she regained her vigor. It was further commanded that I should stay there with her. I was horrified.

Ah, but don't think me idle. I kept trying to find a way to travel west.

Meanwhile, Father, swept up in his enthusiasm (as were so many other Providence men), arranged to sell our house and used some of the money to book passage on a vessel, the *Stephanie K*. A ship of 450 tons, she was scheduled to leave

Providence for California in February of 1849. Father selected sleeping berths that, he said, were big enough for him and Jacob.

"Are these berths big enough to accommodate *me*?" I asked, making one final plea to be included.

Father replied, "Tory, as I have told you many times, you must remain in Providence with Mother."

I did not ask again.

Happily, there was another *magnificent* idea in *Jane Eyre,* which came to my rescue. I beg you to go to chapter 34 and find this sentence. It reads:

I would always rather be happy than dignified.

This unfearing sentiment was the key to solving my difficulty.

Recall: Jacob and I had been conspirators in the matter of my schooling for some time, so we knew how to do things without our parents' knowledge. Is there anything sweeter than siblings' secrets?

Also, had I not joined the library on my own? Had I not been reading secretly? Studied school in secret? Walked alone to downtown Providence?

The plan I devised was simple: when the *Stephanie K.* left Providence, I would be on board—as a stowaway.

·5·

WHEN I TOLD MY BROTHER WHAT I INTENDED to do, he became a willing—if wide-eyed—accomplice. I also think he felt better knowing that I would be with him in California.

Still, my plan had considerable risks.

I might be noticed by my father and put ashore.

Being a stowaway, I might be accused of a crime and the captain might lock me up in the ship's brig, thereby bringing shame to myself and my family.

I might so distress my mother as to set back her recovery.

I might be discovered by the crew of the *Stephanie K.* and once at sea tossed overboard and (God preserve me) drown.

Worst of all? I might fail in my endeavor and be forced to remain in dull Providence with my aunt.

But I had read widely. Thus I had also come upon what that great American Benjamin Franklin wrote: "Nothing ventured, nothing gained."

I presumed that most passengers on the ship would be men. Would I not be able to steal my way aboard by being dressed as a young man? Did that make me uneasy? Fearful? Of course! But I, choosing happiness rather than dignity, was so determined to go to California that I pushed all such worrisome thoughts away.

How was I to do it?

Recall that I had been able to save my earnings, such as they were. Recall that Father had refused them. My honest wages became my means to find my dishonest way.

Once again, I ventured into town. This time, with Jacob at my side, I searched out a shop in the Providence business district that sold used articles of clothing. I told the shop clerk that I wished to purchase inexpensive work clothing for my (nonexistent) *older* brother.

"Since he is about my height," I added, "and I being tall for my age, I can try them on."

The shop assistant eyed me with a blatant suspicion, but I explained: "My brother is too busy working to come himself."

I bought a man's collapsible tall hat, shirt, trousers, jacket, and boots and carried them away. They were previously used, and visibly so, but that only added to their value. A disguise does best when dingy. As soon as we returned home, it was easy enough to stow the clothing at the *bottom* of Jacob's trunk.

With my masquerade at hand, my scheming was almost done. All I needed to do was wait for Father to embark upon the *Stephanie K.* and sail to California.

But there was one other precarious thing which I had to do: I must tell Mother about my intentions.

Why did I have to tell Mother? Because I could not simply *vanish*. My disappearance would upset her to the extreme and be harmful to her health. No, she needed to know about the secret enterprise upon which her courageous daughter was embarking.

But what if she said no?

It was a hazard I had to risk. If a girl *must* put faith in *one* person, it should be her mother.

By then, our house having been sold, Mother and the rest of us were installed in my aunt's house on Benefit Street. Stuffed as it was with heavy furniture in drab colors, heavy drapes at the window made it feel as if we were living in a dim and crowded mausoleum. There, Father all but waited on my aunt, always agreeing with whatever she said. It made me ill.

Then too, Aunt Lavinia checked my clothing daily, looked to see if my hands were clean, asked me what I intended to do each hour.

"You are not my mother," I protested, often.

"Your weak mother is ill because of your foolish father."

If I required any more motivation to escape Providence, my aunt supplied it every moment of every day.

Finding a time when Mother and I were alone — she resting in bed, her red shawl around her, me holding her hand — I told her what I had conspired.

As I revealed my plan to her, she looked at me with astonishment, until the moment came when she outright cried. "And do you," she said, "truly think you can do this?"

"I will do it," I said, working hard to show only eagerness, not my private unease.

"Won't you be in great danger?"

"Father will be there, and of course, Jacob will be too."

"But—"

"Mother, you know how Aunt Lavinia stridently disapproves of me, everything I do and say. She makes this a distressed household, a source of continual irritation to your health. And remember," I reminded her, "you originally agreed that I should go with Father."

Mother did not contest my view. Rather she said, "But what could I tell your aunt as to your whereabouts?"

"Tell her that at the last moment Father changed his mind and brought me along.

"Mother," I pressed, "remind her that Father and Jacob know nothing of housekeeping, cooking, nor cleaning. I can do all those things. She will approve of that. Besides, we both know I am of no use to you here."

Then I added my decisive argument: "Mother, I prefer to be happy rather than dignified."

Mother smiled and squeezed my hand as much as her strength allowed. "Young ladies today," she said, "are much more daring than they were when I was your age. Yes, I can see you being of assistance to Father and Jacob. They will certainly need a woman to run our fine new home."

That was hardly my desire or plan, but once again I kept my thoughts to myself.

I went down on my knees and put my hands in a prayerful position. "Mother, you will join us as soon as possible. In my heart, I believe all will go well. May I?"

She gazed at me for a long while with sad but loving eyes. Then, with much tenderness, she said, "Happy the mother who can admire her daughter. I give permission."

I leaped up and hugged her. Then she unwrapped her favorite red shawl from her shoulders and presented it to me. "Wear it so I can always embrace you."

In other words, Mother agreed to keep my secret. Of course, having a clandestine plan is one thing. Putting it to work was quite another.

·6·

FEBRUARY 12, 1849.

If you have never taken part in the departure of a great ocean sailing ship, I pity you. One cannot begin to comprehend the commotion and exhilarating chaos that prevails. It is like a Fourth of July and New Year's Eve in one, and in my view, all great changes in life should be celebrated.

Consider the Providence wharf that cold and blustery day, with bits of confetti-like snow flecking the air: Crowds of people going on and off the great three-masted ship *Stephanie K.* People joyfully or tearfully wishing one another well. People with faces full of sorrow. People with faces full of glee. People engaged in heart-clinging farewells. People making hasty goodbyes, as if separation could not come fast enough. On the wharf, men's tall hats so numerous it was like a city of smokeless chimneys.

Faces full of expectations. Faces full of dread. Faces pale. Faces flushed. Tears and laughter bucketing from the same hearts. Need I say more? An entire encyclopedia of emotions.

Or, if you prefer (as I did) a perfect melodrama, complete with music, for there on the wharf was a church choir that sang an optimistic hymn that God should bless us all.

There was, too, all manner of cargo—trunks, bales, and boxed belongings—which needed to be brought aboard. Food and water were likewise carried on.

Of course, midst the mingling multitudes of immigrants was the sailing crew, which for the *Stephanie K.* numbered thirty-two, plus officers, including a captain with an elegant black beard.

In other words, a swirling, swarming, and scintillating ship.

The anticipation was intoxicating. Even I, who *never* touched ardent spirits, knew that.

Father, being forty-nine years of age, looked to be the oldest passenger. Most of the travelers on board—there were about one hundred and seventy in total—were young men going to California for gold. Gold fever at the highest temperature. Indeed, the word "gold" buzzed in my ears as if I were standing amidst a swarm of bees in search of summer's golden nectar.

On board, there were only a few women and fewer children. That, I admit, gave me new feelings of trepidation. But I was bolstered by a resolve that was churning like a nor'easter about to burst.

Father and Jacob had made their leave-takings to Mother at her bedside in my aunt's house. Those moments were truly tender, with as much sentiment and clear declarations of love as my parents were capable of expressing.

"Dear wife, I shall think of you often."

"Beloved husband, I shall pray for your success."

In secret, I had made my own goodbyes to Mother the night before. I think Mother had begun to relish this family intrigue as much as I did. I rather suspect she was finding being a convalescent—under the imperial eye of her sister—ever drearier.

Indeed, Mother, now very much wishing to travel west, spoke of embarking on one of the fast new clipper ships as soon as she could. As for the undoubted assurance of my father's great wealth to come, it lifted her spirits and was a buffer against Aunt Lavinia.

"Come as quickly as you can," I urged her.

"Everything will be better there," she said, as much to herself as to me.

"Dearest Mother, thank you for believing in me. Know that I shall always have you in my thoughts and heart."

On the day of departure, I accompanied Father and Jacob upon the *Stephanie K.* There was no hindrance to my boarding since many people were going on to say goodbye to passengers. Midst all that churning of emotions and embraces, no one questioned why I was there.

Once on board, as planned, I asked that Jacob be allowed to show me the sleeping place Father had reserved.

"Of course," said Father.

In haste, my brother led me below. I quickly learned that upon these large ships there is the main deck and the bottom hold, wherein cargo is carried. Between these two areas was the "tween deck," where passengers had their belongings and sleeping compartments.

I was surprised that these compartments consisted of nothing more than what looked like crudely constructed shelves for library books, the shelves hardly more than twenty-five inches wide. All the same, I was much relieved to see Jacob's luggage stowed there, in particular his trunk, which contained my disguise. I now knew where I could find it. When Jacob and I saw the trunk, we exchanged self-assured, conspiratorial grins.

"Where is the ladies' dressing room?" I asked.

"I've no idea," he returned.

While that unnerved me considerably, there was absolutely no time to pause and investigate, so we hastened back to the main deck. Once there, the three of us—Father, Jacob, and

I—went to the gangway, where I spoke what I hoped *sounded* like heartfelt adieus to both Father and Jacob.

As soon as that was accomplished, I walked down the gangplank to the wharf, turned back, and waved a flamboyant farewell. After they, in turn, saluted me, I took a few steps away.

Immediately Jacob did as I had instructed him. He pulled at Father's greatcoat and dragged him away to see some far corner of the great ship. Then came the most *thrilling* moment—up to that time—of my entire life.

I rushed *back* onto the ship via the same footbridge. Once on board, I raced down to Jacob's berth. Had I not learned the way? But since I had not discovered where the women's quarters were, and with my heart beating like an uncaged bird, I had no choice but to open Jacob's trunk and withdraw from its bottom the clothing I had purchased.

The tween deck was teeming with people—passengers, families, and crew bidding farewell. Thus it was that no one cared when I flung a blanket over myself. Beneath it, I dressed as a man, in trousers, shirt, and boots, my long chestnut hair stuffed into a black top hat which sat low upon my brow. When I stepped free and assayed my appearance, I had to suppress my glee as to how I must look. Did ever a girl's heart flutter so?

Leaving my girl's attire in Jacob's trunk, I returned to the main deck, there to mingle among the multitudes of young men. Let it be said: it is fine to be noticed, but it is *delightful* to be *invisible*.

Warning whistles began to be piped. Ship departure! Passengers who were embarking lined the rails and waved to those who retreated to the wharf.

At the library in Providence, I had read Mr. Poe's story "The Purloined Letter," which had impressed me with the idea that the best hiding place is right in the open. I, therefore, remained at the top rail in full view—in my costume, of course—and waved to people on the dock as *if* saying goodbye to kin. Sure enough, although I stood boldly before all, I went completely unnoticed.

Despite the snow, the crew climbed the rigging like sprightly spiders. Sails—from flying jib (at the bow) to spanker (at the stern) to main royal (the topmost sail)—were loosed and sheeted home. The lines that bound the *Stephanie K.* to the east coast of the United States were cast off. Our ship was warped into Narragansett Bay. Having wind and tide in our favor, off we went. *It was absolutely thrilling* so that I fairly tingled with delight. No one—save my brother, Jacob—knew I was a stowaway.

I suppose it is immodest to say, but I was exceedingly pleased with myself. There I was, engaged in a true adventure. None of my mother's romance books equaled this. I was the heroine in my own story.

We sailed down Narragansett Bay with a colony of seagulls as our airborne escort. To my ears, their squawks sounded as if they were laughing with glee, echoing my own delight. Above, the bulky, billowy sails were our own soufflé of clouds. With the bay waters smack-smooth, there was little in the way of disturbing movement.

Shortly after we embarked, all passengers were called on deck, and the captain welcomed us by reading out his rules.

> "All passengers must rise by seven a.m. unless excused by the ship's doctor. Bedtime is no later than ten p.m. No breakfast until all decks are swept and your bedding stowed. No liquor allowed. The use of gunpowder is strictly prohibited. A religious service will be held every Sunday morning by our chaplain. All are required to attend. My first mate shall make sure these rules are enforced."

You may easily imagine how impatient I was, but I had to stay in disguise until we were fully out to sea. Mind, I needed to hide for only the first two days of a seven-month voyage. It greatly helped that during those first days the ship was in a state of continual disarray as passengers learned their way about. In addition, the *Stephanie K.* was fairly packed with young men, a great many of whom were beardless youths, and since I did not look so different from them, I went unnoticed. To further support my ruse, I refrained from speaking, not wishing to reveal my feminine voice.

Jacob and I had planned where and when to meet. At these appointed moments, he brought not just a friendly face but food, drink, and, at our first meeting, a blanket. Yes, I might have eaten at the common tables, but I preferred to take extra precautions.

For me, the next forty-eight hours were the most challenging. We sailed down Narragansett Bay, twixt Point Judith and Newport, and then out upon the awe-inspiring Atlantic Ocean.

I slept those first two nights on deck—one among many sleepers. To be sure, I was cold, but I learned that if you are going to be a heroine in your own adventure, a certain amount of discomfort is obligatory.

At last, we reached the open sea. By day, oh, the sublime endless wonder of it. No land in sight, only ceaseless blue and white-capped foaming waves. Sails fluffed and snapped as the ship hissed and spanked through the wash. By night, a vast array of frozen stars.

As we sailed, we pitched, bobbed, rolled, and yawed enough to make some people ill. Father was one of those, but I am glad to report, not me. To the contrary, my healthy heart fairly swelled in an attempt to match the immensity of the ocean, a seemingly endless world. How shall I best express it? I loved myself for loving it all. If I could, I would have hugged the universe.

After two days had passed, I met with Jacob. He managed to maneuver Father out of his berth, where he lay in sea-sick discomfort. Once he left, I once again ducked beneath a blanket—this time to change back into my young woman's attire.

When I emerged, no one took particular notice of me, appearing as the girl I truly was, in a modest trimmed bonnet and a full-length, high-necked dress, with wide sleeves at my wrists. I also wore Mother's red shawl. As if indifferent—but hardly so—I walked about the main deck until I spied Father standing by the bulwark rail, gazing out upon the sea, per-haps pondering the immense change in *his* life—and in his unhappy belly.

I paused, relishing the moment. Oh, such wonderful drama. When the curtain lifts, is it not delightful to be on center stage?

"Sir!" I called to him. "Mr. Blaisdell!"

·7·

FATHER TURNED AND LOOKED AT ME WITHOUT comprehension. It was that curious truth: the familiar in an unfamiliar place is oft unseen.

It took some full moments before he grasped that it was me. When he did realize it *was* his daughter who stood before him, she whom he thought he'd left behind in Providence, his face displayed complete bewilderment.

"What . . . what," he stammered, "are *you* doing here?"

I almost said, "My will has decided my destiny." Instead, I replied, "I am going to San Francisco."

Father, perfectly dumbfounded, managed to say, "But how . . . how did you *get* here?"

I told him.

"Does Mother know?"

"She approved."

"Did she?" he cried, newly aghast and, I suspect, feeling somewhat betrayed. "But . . . but what do you intend to *do* in California?"

"I'm quite sure, Father, that you can care for yourself. For my part, I intend to take care of Jacob and keep our fine new house. Meanwhile, you shall be free to gather that abundant gold. At dinnertime each day, I shall serve you your meal and you shall regale us with your daily adventures and your new wealth."

These words, though surely stilted, had been well practiced to soothe his ear. I had composed them with that goal in mind.

But though that is what I *said,* let it be clearly understood: *my* vision of my future was to be far more energetic than that. I cared little for gold. My desire was to become fully independent, have intelligent people around me, and somehow (I was not exactly sure) amaze the world. I had already learned that for a girl, the more ambitious you are, the better it is to keep it within.

What did my father do when he realized that I was on the ship and that there was no way he could send me home? He did what many people do when confronted with something that they can't control: he acted as if it was *always* meant to be. What's more, the constant degree of congestion on the ship was such that no one in authority ever realized I was dodging a fare. You may be sure Father was too embarrassed to acknowledge it.

There was something more: I do believe Father looked upon me with the realization that I was far more capable than he had thought before.

That pleased me.

But now that I had resumed my female garb, I was confronted with another problem. As I learned, there were *no* separate accommodations for females.

The ship's chaplain, who was migrating to California, was traveling with his wife. No doubt because of his calling, they had their own tiny cabin beneath the rear deck. As for the two other wives on board, one with a little boy, they simply shared bunks with their respective spouses. As for other girls my age, there were *none*.

I will be the first to admit that this was a circumstance to which I had given no thought. Further, no complaint could be made to the ship's captain because, to begin with, I had no business being on board. And, as I have said, my father and I were not going to draw attention to my dishonest presence.

However, considering how passengers were lodged on that tween deck, my being there proved no great difficulty. Jacob and I shared a shelf—head to toe, toe to head. Father—with a gallantry I had not expected—took his sleep on the deck planking, with no softening save some blankets. We slept in our regular clothing.

But the ship's owners, seeking to maximize profits by the flood of passengers seeking gold in California, had booked far more people than the shelf-beds they had hastily constructed to accommodate them. Thus people were truly aswarm, on their berths, on the deck, in every nook, cranny, and corner of the ship, wherever they could sleep, sit, or stand. Since the little light that existed on the tween deck came from a few lantern lights, one had the impression of a dark, crowded church, with barely a clear vision as to who was next to you.

Nor did it smell good, being stenchy and close. Though all were required to clean their spaces, it remained a filthy place. Hardly a wonder, then, that when the weather was bright, fair, and mild—and even when it was not—many a passenger (including me) spent their days on the main deck breathing the unsullied sea air.

When I needed to change my clothes, the chaplain's wife was kind enough to provide me—and the two other women—moments of privacy in her cabin.

However thrumming the departure of a great ship might be and the undeniable adventure of being a stowaway, the seven-*month* voyage of the *Stephanie K.* which followed was, I fear, tenfold tedious. The truth is, our voyage was disappointingly dull to the extreme. If I were to describe it in *full* detail, you would put these pages down and never return. Would you enjoy reading:

FEBRUARY 20: *Sailed six knots.*

FEBRUARY 21: *Sailed seven knots. Spied ship on the distant horizon.*

FEBRUARY 22: *Sailed three knots. Saw nothing but waves. They were much the same.*

I trust you will agree that it is wise that I don't share every moment of my voyage with you.

But you should know some details.

The ship: The decks never stayed level or still but continually shifted, so that the timbers (like old people's bones) forever groaned and creaked.

Food: It was grim. Salted meats, hard biscuits, beans, and bad-tasting water. Eating times at the two long common tables on the tween deck were raucous, with displays of truly appalling manners.

Passengers: Endlessly impatient, constantly complaining about crowded conditions and our slow speed, criticizing the captain no matter what he did, forever arguing amongst themselves about matters mostly minor.

Some things were unusual: I received *fourteen* offers of marriage. When the first came—from a tall gentleman with an enormous mustache—I was shocked. When the second proposal came — from a dandy with the smell of rose perfume suffusing the air — I was puzzled. By the *fourteenth* proposal, I could only laugh. Naturally I refused them all.

I didn't tell Father of these offers. I did tell Jacob, and I do believe it began to alter his vision of me. It is one thing to have an older sister. It is quite another to have a *married* sister. It was as if only then did he realize our lives would be different. But then, I think boys think far less about the future than girls.

Regarding amusements, whenever I saw someone reading a book, particularly a multivolume novel — which was more often than you might expect — I made bold to inquire if, when they were done, I might borrow it. Thus I read fine new publications such as *Oliver Twist, Wuthering Heights,* and *Vanity Fair,* books different one from the other, but good and happily long. I extended the time of reading by sharing them aloud with Jacob.

In fact, almost all my time was spent in Jacob's company. But then, I hold that the more one loves another — as Jacob and I do — the less reason there is for *talk.* Silence is a form of tranquility. Beware companions who *require* talk. *Being together* should be enough.

So it was that for many a long hour and days Jacob and I leaned against the bulwark rail and did little more than gaze upon the endless gray-blue sea. At night, I read him books by lantern light until we slept.

To be sure, during the voyage there were moments of interest. Most exhilarating was when it seemed as if the ship were in peril, such as when we passed through what the sailors called the williwaws, the roiling, savage, wintry tempests at the southernmost point of South America. One's life, I decided, is enhanced when embracing danger.

How cold was it when we went around the Horn? Ice crusted the rigging and coated the rails and had to be broken off with mallets. Why, the captain's beard froze so that he had to lean over a heated stove to thaw it out.

Winding our way through those tempestuous channels, it took four men to control the steering. The ship bowled and dipped so, that with no sides on the shelf berths, people rolled out as they slept. One man broke his arm. Many became sick.

Cape Horn, the forlorn bit of land which marked the southernmost spot of South America, rose (I was informed) to twelve hundred feet, and was snow covered.

The captain's skill brought us out into the Pacific Ocean, and we headed north, where the seas gradually became calm and the sun grew warm.

The cities, at which we paused — Rio de Janeiro (Brazil), Callao (Peru) — to take on fresh food and water, were fascinating to see. Quite exotic. But only I seemed interested. The truth is there was little concern upon the *Stephanie K.* for *anything* other than San Francisco and gold. If anticipation were riches, we would already have been the wealthiest ship at sea.

I admit I too spent much time imagining what lay before me: I thought of San Francisco as a city of prodigious beauty set upon a picturesque bay (so it had been described), a metropolis full of riches and *elegant* things, altogether serene with strong, handsome—and dare I say it—wealthy people. It was oft called El Dorado, recalling that mythical city of fabulous wealth. This is to say, I populated the city with every bit of my wistful imagination.

As for *where* the easy gold might be found, I envisioned a stately forest, with wide, earthy paths bordered with glittery nuggets of gold, which I gathered like dropped ripe apples. Quickly our family life would be endowed with fabulous riches like those in the finest fairy tales.

But, as we were coming up the west coast of Mexico—drawing ever nearer to our goal of California—things began to change for me yet again in a major way.

·8·

FATHER SAT JACOB AND ME DOWN NEAR OUR berths on the tween deck. We were hardly alone: many passengers were sleeping or sitting about us playing cards, reading, or talking. As the ship rolled and pitched, the whale-oil lamps that dangled from the ceiling swung like clock bobs, causing shadows to leap about us like agile acrobats.

"I have learned some things of great importance," Father began. "As you know, we are approaching San Francisco. I have been talking with some of the men who will be going to the mines. Everybody agrees upon some things.

"The first thing: the gold will *not* be found in San Francisco. One must go some eighty or more miles along the bay to what are called the diggings. Obviously I must go there.

"The second: Tory, it will be unwise for you to go to these diggings with me. The conditions there, I've been reliably informed, are not at all suitable for a girl. I thought I'd easily find us a house there. I have learned such homes do not even exist.

"Also, people insist that it would be just as big a mistake to leave you, Tory, alone in San Francisco. Therefore, Jacob shall stay with you. While I go to reap my share of gold, you two must stay behind in the town, together."

"Left behind?" cried Jacob.

I too protested. "But these men you've talked to have never been to San Francisco or the mines. How could they know what the conditions are?"

"I assure you," said Father, "they know much more than you. And may I remind you, dear Victoria, that you were not invited to come. You chose," he said in a lowered voice, "to make your way upon this ship on your own. I trust that the same strength of character will guide you in San Francisco.

"Beyond all else, I feel it's my obligation to gather wealth before Mother comes. She deserves that. And I intend to prove myself to Aunt Lavinia."

"But—"

"I am your father" was his closing argument. "You are my daughter. Therefore, you shall do as I say."

"Dear Father—"

"Of course," he continued with barely a pause, "I'm informed that San Francisco is a fine, modern city. Before I go to the mines, I promise you I'll find a suitable house and provide sufficient funds so you may take care of it. I shall hire a servant. I'll enroll Jacob in a good school. Don't forget, I have every expectation that Mother will arrive not long after we get there. You'll need to be there to welcome her. The truth is, her health may require it. The three of you can wait in perfect leisure for me to come back with my fortune. Then we shall have what we once had— and more."

Father adamantly refused to listen to any objections from Jacob or me. In other words, while he went to gather his gold, Jacob and I must remain in San Francisco, *alone*.

How did I feel about this proposal? When first I heard it, I went to the main deck and, with Mother's red shawl around me, stared angrily out at the sea. But the more thought I gave to Father's decision, the more my temper shifted from vexation to consent to delight. Belatedly, I realized, I was being given the opportunity to prove how truly independent I was. I would live in *total* freedom. I could not ask for more.

Once I embraced this unexpected independence, I was full of eager anticipation. For the first time in my life, I would— excepting Jacob—live alone.

As for taking care of my brother, I thought nothing of it.

We remained as close as siblings could be. We would have no conflicts. School must take up most of Jacob's time. I assumed we would have a servant to attend to his needs. While that happened, I intended to live free, far freer than in Providence. Let me further confess: I began to think how wonderful our new wealth would be. In other words, I could hardly wait to arrive. We had only to reach San Francisco for my full liberation to take place.

We continued to sail up the Mexican coast—as we were informed, for we could not see it—drawing ever closer to the city of San Francisco. Alas, the trade winds were such that we had to go far north and west, as if heading for the Sandwich Islands, then tack about so as to sail south and east.

Just as we reached our long-anticipated goal—it was August 1849, and we had been at sea for *six months*—we were again thwarted. A thick fog obscured the California coast. While our captain insisted we were close to the narrow entry known as the Golden Gate, which would lead us into San Francisco Bay and the fabled city, that passage was not easily located. The captain likened his task to threading a needle. To proceed without precision, he announced, was extremely dangerous. What's more, the flow of tide in and out through this Golden Gate was famously fierce. We might, he warned us, be wrecked.

To be sure, the captain took pains to tell us that those

within the bay were no doubt just as frustrated about getting *out* since the fog inside was probably just as dense there.

It was all wonderfully emotive. Shadowy fog. Hidden vistas. Possible wreckage. The true exhilaration of travel. All we lacked were pirates.

In any case, we were forced to sail back and forward, north and then south, for *five* days, trying to avoid, on one side, the rocky off-coast Farallon Islands, while we tried to find, on the other side, the Golden Gate, the way into the great San Francisco Bay, and the fabulous fields of gold.

As you might expect, after such a lengthy voyage, my anticipation was high. Jacob and I stood (with many other impatient passengers) upon the deck and stared out day after day, hour by hour, into the wet and swirling ashen air. I, for one, found the thick fog to be wonderfully haunting. What wonders was it concealing? Oh, the sweet suspense.

Yes, it was frustrating. Still, is there not something sublime in frustration when you know that joy must arrive shortly? It is like a coming birthday; you know a present will be given to you, but you can't bring the date forward.

"There! There!" someone would call as the fog lifted momentarily. Brown and green promontories appeared. A log upon the sea. A leafy branch. Then, oh, the sighs of dismay from all when, next moment, everything became lost to view and the miasma reclaimed the world.

At last, however, the haze melted. A lovely buttery sun revealed itself on high. The sky was blue. Midst enormous excitement and the highest expectations, we sailed *through* the Golden Gate, with its jagged and steep cliffs to either side. How awe-inspiring.

Next, the celebrated San Francisco Bay unfolded before us like a fan of paradise. The inland sea was truly immense, big enough to hold *all* the navies of the world. Waters sparkling as if alive. Pods of dolphins cavorted about our bow. Overhead, pelicans barked and gulls squawked their welcome.

We sailed by a high hill, and what appeared to be a small, uninhabited, and rather spectral-looking island, where there were no dwellings, only countless birds.

Then for the first time, there before me, I beheld the celebrated city of San Francisco.

What I saw stunned me.

PROVIDENCE, RHODE ISLAND — THE ONLY CITY
I knew — was a large, *old* metropolis, set upon a graceful
tree-crested hill with a multitude of fine wood, brick, and
stone homes. Dignified office blocks and a busy port with
many wharves were part of its commercial center.

By way of contrast, San Francisco was set amidst steep,
scrubby hills the color of dead straw, with dusty, sandy dunes
and little shrubbery. Its former name was Yerba Buena, Spanish
for "good herb." But those minty-tasting bushes were, for the
most part, gone, replaced by stunted shrubs and a muddle of
low, wretched, lopsided buildings. These pathetic structures
came right down to the water as if they had slid off the hills
into a great jumblement. I observed but one small wharf, plus

a few others being constructed. What a dismal, quilt-without-color vista!

Though we approached a landing cove, perhaps a mile wide, our ship was required to anchor many yards from shore because the waters were so shallow. I could see, and worse, *smell*, broad flats of obnoxious mud. Even more remarkable, within the cove, as though *stuck* in that mud, were great numbers of ships. They appeared altogether abandoned: a fleet of ghostlike vessels.

But before I could make sense of what I was seeing, our noble captain, after six months of sailing, cried out, "Stand clear. Let go anchor!"

What followed was something close to a riot, while almost two hundred passengers, so long confined, in near pandemonium, clamored to get off. It was as if people believed fist-size gold nuggets lay upon the nearby beach, and all were determined, nay, desperate, to claim their share. What's more, not only did the passengers rush to disembark, but the *entire* crew—captain included—also left. They too, some with their sea chests on their shoulders, were in quest of gold.

One hears the expression "rats abandoning a sinking ship." Though we were *not* sinking and I did not *see* any rats leaving, we were, nonetheless, left behind. It seemed that no one wished to have anything more to do with the steadfast *Stephanie K.* The promised gold upon the land was the only desire.

Yet none of the passengers could walk off. They had to be carried ashore by a flotilla of large rowboats called lighters. Multi-oared, these boats rushed out to meet us and poked about our hull like so many nursing piglets. Furthermore, the men who rowed these lighters implored our custom and asked—nay, *demanded*—whether we had goods to sell. Then, to be carried to shore, these same rowers—better to call them thieves—insisted upon payment of three or five dollars. It was but our first experience of the extraordinary cost of living in San Francisco.

Though Father managed to disembark, he told Jacob and me to remain on board while he went ashore to find and rent a fine house in which we might live.

"Be patient," he said. "I want to make sure we have a graceful home."

It did not take long before our ship was mostly emptied of people: no crew or officers remaining and almost no passengers. The *Stephanie K.*'s sails hung limp, her deck littered with discarded things, from boots to barrels. Jacob and I could have taken possession of the ship and sailed her to China if we'd had the skills. Having no such talent, there was little for us to do but to stare at this strange place called San Francisco.

I was looking at a city—as I would later learn—made of prefabricated wood-frame houses with cloth (or paper) walls, lopsided packing boxes converted into homes, a few brick and adobe houses, plus flimsy wood houses from China. There were even peculiar *iron* houses from New York. *Proper* buildings were rare. No elegant squares.

Nothing I observed of the city appeared attractive. San Francisco seemed to consist, mostly, of a multitude of sail-cloth tents of different colors. *Tents. Thousands* of them. I was reminded of a large revival meeting camp. Yet I knew perfectly well it was gold the inhabitants were seeking here, not God. Truth to tell, I saw not one church spire. I would learn later than even our ship's chaplain and his wife had set off for the gold mines.

No, I observed not a hint of the *extraordinary* fabled wealth. The *worst* of Providence seemed vastly more refined than the *best* of San Francisco. The word *style* could hardly be used here—surely not by me. The land of glittering gold revealed itself as mostly rich in rubbish.

Let it be admitted, when one has been foolish enough to believe a myth, one casts more anger upon the myth than upon the fool (oneself!) who believed it.

"Are we really going to live here?" Jacob asked me, his voice full of disbelief.

For once my natural enthusiasm was so dimmed, I could only manage to say, "I fear so."

It was six long hours before Father returned. He came back, as he had gone, in one of those lighters. During that time, the prospect that lay before us became worse. The empty vessels remained but the tide had receded, so the mudflats had become further uncovered. These flats were full of small channels, which looked like wet snakes. And the stink was extreme.

"Come along," Father called up to us. "I have arranged that our belongings will be brought later."

Jacob shouted down with renewed excitement, "Have you found us a home?"

"I have."

"Is it bigger than we had on Sheldon Street? Shall I have a large bedroom of my own?"

"You will see," said Father, but I detected something in his voice that gave me unease.

"What about food?" I asked.

"Of course."

We were rowed to shore. The boatman, an old, grizzled fellow, with long-fingered, blue-veined hands and a battered top hat on his head, rowed his way through the twisty channels, maneuvering among those lifeless ships I'd previously observed. These fully masted ships were huge, towering over our heads, pressed one upon another, as I might imagine a desperate naval battle but without so much as one cannon boom. Instead there was an altogether alarming lack of life.

Puzzled, I stared up at the gigantic vessels: multimasted fighting ships, barques, merchant ships, schooners, and brigs.

There appeared to be *hundreds* of them. Yet all appeared derelict.

"Why are these ships here?" I asked the man who was rowing us.

"Discarded," he said with a shrug. "The crews have gone off to the gold fields."

"Just *left* the ships?" asked Jacob, eyes wide with wonder.

"Nobody wants them," said our rower. "Help yourself if you'd like." He gave a gap-toothed grin and nodded at Jacob. "You can be captain."

Sure enough, I observed signs nailed to the hulls of a few ships that read FOR SALE or FREE.

As we wended our way, the forsaken ships bumped and banged one against another, creaking, rattling, and groaning. Some of them had begun to be stripped and torn apart. Others lay half sunk. It was all as extraordinary as it was grotesque: a fleet of ghostly hulks. But if they *were* apparitions, they were of a singular sort, for they threw off a strong stench, rather like bad cheese mixed with brackish seawater.

Jacob pinched his nose so hard, its tip went white. I could only think, *I want nothing to do with this.*

Our rower, who must have seen the look of amazement on our faces, grinned and said, "Folks are calling these ships Rotten Row."

·10·

W E REACHED THE BEACH, DISEMBARKED, THEN
walked across the sandy waterside. To do so we had to
sidestep discarded carpetbags, crates, casks, and bales, plus
sacks of what appeared to be spilled coffee and spoiled flour.
Beyond that, we reached a wide mud path.

"Montgomery Street," Father announced.

A street? Barely. Not one cobblestone, but merely dirt,
reduced in many places to a muddy quagmire. In wonder, I
reached down to touch the gummy sludge. This slubber was
everywhere, two, and sometimes three feet deep. I, who was
too often like a spouting dictionary, was reduced to muteness.

As far as I could see, San Francisco did not have any *real*
streets, nothing like Providence. Instead, lanes two feet wide

wound among a hodgepodge of shops, eating houses, plus whatever people called home.

There were gambling establishments *everywhere* I looked, a quantity sufficient to challenge my mathematical reckoning. Nor could I begin to count how many drinking places— saloons and doggeries—I observed. The air was heavy with whiffs—no, rather *clouds*—of whiskey vapor.

As for my ears, they were filled with a constant clamor, sounds of squabbling voices, shouts, and sometimes disturbing screams.

Many shops had signs telling what they sold, but in such a litany of languages, I could not begin to guess what they offered. I had the odd sensation that we had arrived not in a different country but in *many* different countries, all squashed together. In short, my senses—sight, hearing, and touch—were disordered. My primary state of mind, bepuzzlement.

All the same, Jacob and I followed Father up a steep hill, which he chose to call Sacramento Street. In so doing, we were required to avoid broken tubs and chests as well as thrown-away goods and rubbish, including what appeared to be a discarded open iron safe. The lack of storage space, Father explained, required goods to be stored outside. Theft, he assured us— I cannot say *how* he knew—was rare.

A few sections of the muck-covered streets had narrow

wooden planks upon which to tread. When we stepped on such, they sank into the ooze, with a gross *sucking* sound.

The street filth required me to hold up my skirts, which became grimy anyway. The sludge oozed between my toes, so that my shoes, I was sure, were ruined. In truth, walking proved so difficult, I resolved that when we got to our new house, my man's boots must be used.

To my further disgust, I saw a multitude of scurrying rats, gray, black, and *white* ones with disturbingly pink eyes. Seeing us, these creatures lifted their revolting bewhiskered snouts without fear and sniffed as we passed as if to say, "This is *our* place. What are *you* doing here?"

Adding to this awfulness was a bothersome breeze, which coated all with dust, enough to thicken my hair. I could *feel* it happen, and resolved to wash it as soon as possible.

To add to everything, the city truly stank.

As we went on, we continually had to make our way through crowds that consisted of mostly men. It made me feel odd. What kind of world had I come to? Had women and girls been banished? Yes, the passengers on the *Stephanie K.* had been almost all males. But here was a *city* of men. And none appeared older than thirty years of age. I confess it gave me considerable unease.

These men were *not* attractive. Each man different perhaps, but all had in common dirty, ill-kempt beards along with uncut hair that made them look like shabby porcupines. They also dressed much the same: broad-brimmed slouch hats, red or blue flannel shirts, and corduroy trousers tucked into heavy boots. What's more, they carried either a Colt pistol or a bowie knife in their belts, sometimes both. It was as if the city were occupied by a bandit army. There were many others who dressed in somewhat different fashion — I supposed Mexicans and Chinese — and who spoke their own language.

"Who are all these men?" I asked.

"Miners," murmured Father.

Have I made myself clear? I was aghast by all I saw. Where, I wondered, was the spirit of gentle Saint Francis, from whom the city took its name? I confess my courage faltered. I could all but hear, "What would Aunt Lavinia say to this?"

In haste, I scolded myself; I was in San Francisco, thousands of miles from Providence. This was the destiny my will had given me. There was no way I could go back. We would get to our new house, and I would hide away.

Jacob, also struggling through the mud, called out, once, twice, three times, "Are we close?"

Father said, "We need to reach California and Stockton Streets."

I was finding it hard to believe that there were *any* such streets when Father abruptly announced, "Here we are: home."

Baffled, Jacob and I looked around.

"What do you mean?" I asked. "Where? What?"

"Right in front of you," said Father. "This tent."

A tent!

The tent Father pointed to was made of what appeared to be old brown sailcloth, patched enough to have been a beggar's cloak. Its roof was held up by a crooked wooden branch in the middle so that it was some five feet in height. Its walls were kept down by stakes. The inner floor—no more than eight feet by eight feet—was naught but dirt. I was reminded of pictures I'd seen of Egyptian pyramids. It might have been as old.

Yet Father had called it home.

Jacob, his voice as full of shock as were my thoughts, asked, "Are we going to . . . *live* here?"

"Until," said Father, "I return from the gold fields and purchase something better. It cost only a hundred dollars." He spoke with pride, as if he had made a great bargain.

As I would learn, he had.

Let it be said, there were many other tents to all sides of ours in which people were living.

But not all. Right across from our tent, separated by nothing more than a muddy twenty-foot strip, was what appeared to be an eatery. It was, in fact, a huge wooden box propped up by a number of barrels. Over the open window—there was no door—written words proclaimed: SAN FRANCISCO CAFÉ RESTAURANT.

Standing inside this odd structure, behind a wooden plank, was a man. Rather small, he had a leathery-dark face and black hair, along with a welcome smile.

"Bienvenidos," he called from across the way. "I am Señor Rosales, and I am glad to have you in nuestro barrio. We shall be amigos. Do you speak Spanish? No? ¡Qué triste! It shall be my personal pleasure to teach you." When he spoke, he rolled his *R*s so they rumbled softly, the most pleasing sound to touch my ears since arriving in San Francisco.

Father stepped across the way, shook hands with the man, and introduced himself and us: "Mr. Randolph Blaisdell; my son, Master Jacob; my daughter, Miss Victoria."

"How wonderful," cried the señor. "I have two children as well. But, señor," he said, his voice suddenly filled with caution, "I must tell you: San Francisco is *not* a good place for niños. They are like corderos. Lambs. Not safe. You may be sure, there are lobos about. Wolves. May I offer you some desayuno— breakfast?"

He was being so kind, warning us about the city, giving us lessons in Spanish, and offering breakfast all at once.

"Thank you," said Father. "But we need to move into our new home."

I was in fact quite hungry, but we retreated to that tent— our home.

That home took little time to organize. Furnishings consisted of three beds—blankets over boards—and our baggage, which was soon delivered (at more high cost), plus a discarded biscuit box that Jacob found not far off in the muddy street. He dragged it in and set it down in the middle, where it served for a table.

All too quickly then, the three of us were sitting in that tent, the front flaps down. The air was stultifying, the smell rather like a rank washcloth.

At first no one spoke because—I suspect—we didn't know what to say or do. It was as if we had traveled to X but had come to Y and weren't sure how it happened. That's to say, though we had traveled across the world, we knew not where we were and hardly knew what came next.

The look on Jacob's face was one of great perplexity. Now and again he reached out and touched the tent's cloth wall, as if not believing it was real. Then he would look at Father, then at me, as if we might have something to say.

We did not.

Father, though he tried to hide it, seemed equally unsure of himself. More than once he consulted his pocket watch as if to suggest that he might have an appointment. Most assuredly he did not.

As for me, I was mortified. I realized I had believed in

larger-than-life dreams. I too—I acknowledge—had succumbed to gold fever. Restored to health, I could see that the reality was altogether bizarre.

"Father," I said at last, "I am filthy. How am I to wash? Where do we get water?"

"It will need to be fetched. I shall have to purchase some buckets."

I looked about. "And will I have no privacy?" I said.

"I shall put up a curtain wall."

(Next day Father secured a piece of old sail and strung it across one corner. So much for seclusion. Little that it was, I was thankful for it.)

We continued to sit for a while in silence, each of us, in our own way, no doubt, trying to make sense of where we were.

At length, I said, "Father, what shall happen to us?"

Father pulled himself up, consulted his watch, and said, "I've told you many times: I'll quickly make my fortune in gold and then . . ." He faltered.

"And then . . . *what?*" I said.

He went on to paint an airy picture of the future that seemed to be a replication of what we'd had in Providence, soon to be rebuilt in San Francisco.

A sweep of anger went through me. "Dear Father," I said, speaking, I fear, like a book heroine in excessive distress, "have we come so far, over such a long time, at such great expense and peril, cutting all ties with our past, only to make every-thing exactly what it was before? This world we've come to is . . . is different and new. But different in the most dreadful of ways."

I concluded by saying—nay, demanding—yet again, "What will become of us?"

He was quiet for a moment and then he said, "I have an obligation to your mother to regain our fortunes."

I wanted to say (though did not), *But what about us?* When I realized that he had no answers, I felt a surge of anger. But as we sat there, my anger subsided. Because as I looked at Father, I understood that ire and resentment would do me little good. In its place came the realization that if Jacob and I were to survive, it would be me who needed to care for us. If ever there was a moment when *Your will shall decide your destiny*, this was it.

But let it be said: It is one thing to be transported to a different *place*. It is quite another thing to be transported to a different way of *being*. Had I not wanted change? Well, then, *vast* change was now a necessity. But I had no idea how to make it happen.

·II·

A S WE SOON DISCOVERED, HAVING A TENT HOME in San Francisco was like living atop an anthill that kept having more ants. Each day *hundreds* of new people arrived in San Francisco. During our first weeks in the city, two *hundred* more ships arrived and disgorged their passengers. The vessels were thus added to the fleet called Rotten Row. Daily, fifteen to thirty so-called homes were put up in the city, with people moving into them all but instantly. There were never enough new homes.

Nor was there—while most indelicate, it must be said— any sanitation. Waste was disposed of upon the sandy hills or in the bay. The city stank. We used an earthenware chamber pot. I don't wish to say more.

At the beginning of the year—1849—the city contained less than two thousand citizens. By the time we arrived, there were something like *fifteen* thousand. Gold was the magnet for these souls. It reminded me of the saying "Where industry walks, greed gallops."

Many a newcomer barely came to shore but rushed off in search of gold down-bay to what they called the diggings. These people called themselves Argonauts, after those who sought the Golden Fleece in ancient Greece. To my mind, these California newcomers were being fleeced.

I refused to be.

I took it upon myself to purchase food, only to discover prices were extraordinarily high. For one egg, a dollar! A potato cost seventy-five cents. Water? A dollar a *bucket*. What's more, as we quickly learned, there was no easy access to water. We had to fetch it, *buy* it, and then haul it back to our tent— uphill!

All this meant that I soon came to understand that Father had insufficient money for our needs. That led to the further realization that *I* must secure some money, which is to say, I needed to find work.

As you know, I had worked—discreet ladies' work—in Providence. Would I, a girl, in San Francisco, even be able to find, and what's more, be allowed to undertake, employment?

As it happened, because so many men were at the diggings,

laborers were scarce. That meant it turned out to be easy for me to secure some work. I may have been a tall and skinny girl, but I was strong and — most of all — willing to learn. I had done so before. As long as I could do the tasks required, nobody minded who I was.

There was one major problem. My clothing — my girl's clothing: skirts, blouses, and bonnets — made it difficult to work, and they became constantly dirtied. Washing was, at best, a gross challenge, expensive, and endlessly time-consuming. No wonder so many San Francisco men were filthy. From the moment I put my foot on California soil, I too was soiled. Since I had been raised with one of Aunt Lavinia's favorite maxims, "Cleanliness is next to godliness," this was hard.

I was forced to make the decision: I would have to dress in men's garb. Being so clothed would make it easier to work, and easier to keep somewhat clean. Not truly clean: *somewhat* clean.

I, therefore, purchased baggy corduroy trousers and flannel shirts at Howard & Mellus, a large dry-goods store by the cove. This clothing allowed me to get through deep mud while saving hours of washing chores. It had nothing to do with hiding who I was. It merely allowed me to labor.

Another thing: during my first days in the city, when I walked about in my girl's dress, many a miner approached and rudely asked me to marry him. You may be sure it wasn't love that brought these proposals but, I realized, a desire to have a servant. My man's costume put an end to such absurd insults.

I also kept my hair in one long braid, taking my style from Chinese men.

So it was that within a week of our arrival, I was pushing wheelbarrows through deep mud. I learned to row (about which more later) a borrowed rowboat to help unload newly arrived ships and bring luggage and passengers to land. It paid well, though it did give me (at first) hand blisters. I also helped carpenters or newcomers put up frame houses and cover them with canvas, cotton, or paper.

This is to say I put my hands to whatever paid me. By doing so, I made as much as *ten* dollars a day or more. Ten times more than I had earned in Providence.

Oddly enough, the men for whom I worked paid me with grains of gold, not coin, because there wasn't much real money around. That made me smile: here was Father about to seek gold at the diggings, while I was already acquiring gold by working in the city. I had more wealth than I ever thought possible, much more than Father had at that point. All of this enhanced my sense of freedom.

Doing what was required meant I grew physically and mentally stronger every day while onerous tasks became easier. Here was a new kind of spirited life, a new me. Could any heroine ask for more?

Was this difficult? To be sure. You may believe I was truly required to live the notion *I would rather be happy than dignified.* Let it be admitted, I had little dignity. Let it also be said that I enjoyed the independence.

I think my working—and my way of dressing—was an embarrassment to Father. No doubt he barely recognized me. Well, then, we hardly recognized him.

He started to dress like a miner, complete with red flannel shirt, slouch hat, and boots. He even grew a beard. He spent all his time learning what he must do and where to go while purchasing the tools he needed for the diggings. Father, the most placid of men, now had a bowie knife in his belt. I doubt he ever used it.

In Providence, before he lost his position, he had been, as I previously described him, a careful, nonadventurous man. Announcing that he was now merely days and a little effort away from acquiring colossal wealth, he thought *only* of gold. This was not unusual. If gold fever was an *illness* on the East Coast, in San Francisco it was a universal *plague.*

Beyond all else, Father, who had been a most thoughtful if restrictive parent, now showed us, his children, almost no attention at all. For the most part, he left us alone, telling us he was looking for servants and a school for Jacob.

In all of this, only Jacob stayed the same. Whereas I had begun to work, Jacob was at a loss as to what to do. At first he tried to follow Father about. Father shooed him away. Then he tried to join me where I was working. That too proved impossible. As a result, he wandered aimlessly, though never far from our tent.

It was painfully clear that Jacob much preferred to be taken care of, not wishing to make choices for himself, not willing to bestir himself. I was struck with the truth: that as a sister grows older, her brother seems to grow younger.

The most useful thing Jacob did was befriend our across-the-way neighbor, Señor Rosales. The good man was ever patient as Jacob chattered and tried to help. As for me, Señor Rosales called me corderita, which I understood to mean "little lamb."

A few days before Father headed for the diggings, we sat in the tent around the box that was our table, the sole light coming from a small solitary and smoky candle. As we ate our dinner of slab beef, which I had cooked outside over a fire, Father abruptly turned to me and said, "Tory, I trust you understand, when I leave, it's all well and good that you are working, but your chief responsibility is to take care of Jacob."

Taken by surprise, I echoed, *"Chief?"*

"Of course. You are his sister, four years older than he. That makes *you* in charge. I have tried to hire a servant. None are to be had at the wages we paid back east. And, I am afraid to say, there seems to be no school here."

Let it be said, the notion that henceforward I was to be the *sole* person responsible for Jacob was hardly pleasing to me. Once again, this was not what I had envisioned in coming west.

Jacob's angry face made it clear this was not what he desired either. He argued with Father, begging him to let us go to the gold fields with him. Father refused.

"I'm depending on you," Father continued saying to me, "to take care of your brother. Mother is depending on it. Is that understood?"

No doubt I nodded, but I was thinking not about Jacob, but myself: Here I was, a fourteen-year-old girl who had just begun to enjoy full freedom. Though Jacob surely was my dear brother, I cannot say I wanted to engage my time being a nursemaid to him. Yet I had to acknowledge, this was, in part, my own doing. If I had *not* come to San Francisco, surely Father would have taken Jacob with him. There was nothing I could say. Even so, with Father about to leave us alone in San Francisco, I made an important decision: I would *not* give up my new life for my brother.

·12·

THREE WEEKS AFTER WE ARRIVED IN SAN
Francisco—it was in September—I rowed Father, along
with his shovel, pickax, gold-sifting pans, and other equipment,
across the shallow, smelly waters of Yerba Buena Cove. Jacob
was with us. We were taking Father to the *Senator*, a black-
and-white side-wheeler steamship. She was anchored some
two hundred yards from San Francisco's landing beach, ready
for the ten-hour trip to Sacramento and the gold diggings.

We reached the boat and climbed aboard. Once there,
Father chucked a brooding Jacob under his chin to get him
to look up.

"Keep watching for Mother," he said. "You know how
unpredictable ships are coming from back east. But you

understand, I can't wait for her." (He kept saying this as if he needed to justify his leaving us alone.) "I need to get to the diggings before the gold gives out."

"Mother may well arrive tomorrow," Father continued. "When she gets here, stay with our tent so I can find you. Keep checking the post office. I have to assume she'll write to say on which ship she'll come."

"Now, I have asked Señor Rosales to keep a watch on you. Pay heed to him."

(It wasn't as if Father had become friends with the señor. But the young men who were in tents to either side of us changed frequently, moving in, then moving out, quickly replaced by new miners. But aside from the fact that Señor Rosales was the only one who stayed, I found him to be wise, kind, and generous.)

"I'll return no later than December first," continued Father. "By that time, I'll be rich, and I promise you, I'll build a bigger and better home than our Providence house."

All I said to Father was "Yes, sir." I lacked the courage to tell what I had learned: only a few miners made fortunes. Truth be known, I had more gold in *my* pocket from working in the city than most. What's more, I was weary of Father's empty assurances and lecturing.

Father, who continued to smile through his new beard,

which made him look like a short, pudgy bear, turned again to Jacob and said, "Try not to worry."

To me, he added, "Try and act a little ladylike. Think of what Aunt Lavinia would say."

I no longer did.

Father gripped our shoulders and gave us a final squeeze. "I'm planning," he said, "on all of us having a plum of a Christmas right here in San Francisco."

"Yes, sir," I said.

"Continue to take whatever suitable jobs you can," he said to me, "and be careful with the money I've left you for as long as possible. You should have enough until I get back. Victoria, make sure to keep the money in that belt I got you. Is that clear?"

He leaned forward and in a half whisper added, "I've put a knife in the belt. In case."

A *knife*. The notion frightened me. But then I reasoned that it was what so many San Francisco men had. It was part of the outfit. It might as well be part of mine.

"And here," Father said to Jacob, "is a good-luck pelican feather for you."

I knew my brother well enough to guess his thoughts: *A knife for Tory. A feather for me.*

He had become a sullen boy.

Next moment, the ship blew a whistle blast that snatched me from my thoughts.

"Time for you to get off," said Father, and he shook hands with Jacob and gave me a hug, his new beard scratchy, which I did not like.

As we climbed down the ship's rope ladder, Father leaned over the rail and watched as we got into our borrowed rowboat. It was part of the freedom of San Francisco that rowboats and other small boats were left at the cove beach, and people could borrow them so long as they brought them back.

I took up the oars. Jacob got into the stern seat. Father, standing among the crowd of gold miners who had paid fifteen dollars for deck passage, waved goodbye. There were so many men on the ship that it listed to starboard. Jacob refused to look back, but only gripped the gunwale of our rowboat, muttering crossly to himself.

I began to row us back to the cove beach. There it was: Jacob and I were in San Francisco—alone. How did I feel? Exhilarated. To my knowledge, there was no book that I had read about a girl alone in a wild and wicked city. I was a heroine like no other.

Then I considered Jacob, sitting in the stern, looking small and abandoned. He was an impediment. He had become, I realized, a new anchor.

·13·

"HATE FATHER GOING," JACOB SAID AS I ROWED toward shore.

"That's foolish," I returned, compelled to truly begin being in charge of him. "The whole point of our coming here is so he can gain riches, is it not? And we need to wait for Mother. Correct? Please stop worrying. I promise: Mother will get here soon. Ships are arriving all the time. I heard twenty came in yesterday, among them one from China and two from Chile, as well as ones from England and Australia."

He said, "What about from Rhode Island?"

When I made no answer, he shifted around to seek a last look at Father. "What if Father *doesn't* get any gold?"

Though I knew that was a perfectly fair question, I gave no reply.

"Not everyone gets rich, you know," he said, and took off his hat and studied the feather Father had given him. "And if the feather is so lucky, why did he give it to me? *He's* the one who needs luck.

"Another thing," he went on. "I met this boy just in from back east. Said there's some sickness there. Called . . . cholera."

He was trying to keep from crying.

His list of possible disasters not complete, he said, "What if Mother gets sick? And . . . and I don't like Father's new beard. It scratches."

I said, "All miners have them."

"But what if—?"

I found Jacob so aggravating that I smacked an oar down on the water and splashed his face.

"Jacob Blaisdell," I cried, "don't you know anything? The more you speak 'what if' balderdash, the more likely it'll come true. *Let your will decide your destiny.*"

"What's that mean?"

"You're too young to understand."

Jacob, sulky, wiped water from his face and glared at me. Next moment, his boyish chest heaved with suppressed sobs. Then, in a switch to a sarcastic voice, he cried out, "Nothing bad will happen. *Nothing.*"

Then, in his true voice, he added, "Except I keep thinking that something bad *is* going to happen. But don't listen to *me.*"

"I don't intend to," I snapped. "I am going to enjoy my new life. I urge you to do the same."

As I rowed, I had a keen sense that it was hard being the older sister: hard for me and for Jacob. Did he wish to be independent of me or be under my supervision? I think it was difficult for him to know.

It is curious: the same conditions make people act in different ways. San Francisco's wildness caused Jacob to worry and be wrought with anger. It filled me with energy.

We reached the shore and started walking uphill. Halfway back up to our tent, passing mules, donkeys, and horses pulling wagons, Jacob's left boot stuck in the mud. Frustrated and irate, he twisted around and looked back down at the bay. The morning fog had lifted and a wind was rising, gusting that everlasting dust.

I followed his look. Beyond the four hundred or so ships of Rotten Row, and the dozen newly arrived vessels, I saw the *Senator*. Side wheels churning, she was moving toward the gold fields, leaving a trail of vanishing smoke.

"Tory," said Jacob in a voice full of true despair, "what if Father . . . disappears like . . . like that steamer smoke? People say it happens all the time. The men go up to the diggings, get lost or die. We'd know *nothing*. We'd never hear of Father again. And what if something happens to Mother's ship? If *she* doesn't come? We'd have to stay here—just us. Or . . . or what if something happens to *you*? What would happen to me? I don't want to be alone!" Tears were flowing down his cheeks.

"Jacob, you're like a pincushion with every worry a prickly pin."

"You're not so great!" he cried. "You dress like a boy. You're tall and scrawny with brown hair braided down to the middle of your back. Nothing but a skinny scarecrow. Ugh."

Refusing to let him diminish my spirits, I merely called, "Come on, slowpoke. You heard Father: we're required to stay together."

With a gross *glugging* sound, Jacob pulled his booted foot out of the mud and started to move uphill again.

I had the thought: *What will I do with him?*

·14·

A S DAYS PASSED, JACOB KEPT SAYING THAT IF there were a school, he could make friends. But as Father had discovered, there wasn't any school in San Francisco. A one-room schoolhouse existed near the plaza, but the teacher had—like so many—gone for gold, and the building had been converted into the headquarters for the city police and a jail. Somehow Jacob learned that the Baptist church might open a new school soon. For my brother's sake, and mine, I hoped it would happen.

San Francisco also had no library. How barbaric.

As for the young men of San Francisco, if they had wives and children, they had left them behind, intending to go back as soon as they gained their heaps of gold. As a result, there were only a few boys Jacob's age in town, and most often they had jobs with family businesses—boardinghouses, stores, eating houses, and the like. They were almost always working, as I was.

Jacob did not work. Rather, he grew more despondent. Every day he went to the post office to see if a letter had come from Mother. The sole post office was a one-story wooden building with a front porch on Clay Street above the plaza. There were two places to get mail: *A* to *N* were on that front porch, *O* to *Z* at the side of the building. For some reason, no letters came to the city until October. But even when they did start to come, no letters came for Blaisdell.

While I *always* managed to find employment, it was only now and again that Jacob roused himself to find a little occupation: fetching for carpenters, masons, or washing dishes in Señor Rosales's café. But I admit, he brought in some gold.

Portsmouth Square, or the plaza, as some called it, was the center of the city. It had a flagpole from which hung the United States flag, with its thirty stars. The old Mexican adobe customs house was on the plaza, as was the alcalde's office, which served as city hall. The post office was near.

It was also where the Parker House and the El Dorado, the city's biggest gambling saloons, stood. Every hour of every day they drew wagering and drinking men. The drunken, staggering miners often dropped grains of gold on the big, open, muddy area. Jacob and others (including impoverished men) would go there in search of specks and now and again found some. Since gold might be worth from eight to twenty dollars an ounce, it was worth looking.

"See?" he'd say, showing me his tiny bits. "I make money too."

Yet Jacob, who was smaller, less strong, and, let it be said, less eager to find jobs that engaged him, became bored.

Father had once given him a copper-colored coin—he called it a token. Something from an election. It had a picture of Henry Clay on it, a man who had run for president of the United States. Jacob liked to spin and flip it. He could, and did, spend hours at a time whistling and doing nothing but flipping that coin. If that is not emptiness I know not what it is.

By way of contrast, I engaged with new people, finding new skills, animated by a new life. Though I loved Jacob, in his loneliness, in his homesickness, he clung to me like a barnacle. And just like a barnacle on a ship, Jacob became an increasing drag to me, which, more and more, I resented.

Fortunately, there was Señor Rosales. I told my brother he *must* be of help to the good man in exchange for his kindness to us.

The señor had been a Mexican soldier before the United States annexed California after the war. Not only did he cook in his café, but he lived in it as well. He even slept there in a *coffin*, claiming it kept him dry and was much cheaper than paying ten dollars a week to a crowded, noisy, and filthy boardinghouse. He preferred to send his money to his family in Sonora, which was elsewhere in California.

Señor Rosales had a telescope from the time he was a soldier. He lent it to Jacob, who climbed Goat Hill, the highest point in town, where he spent hours looking at the incoming ships in hopes that Mother was on one of them. Not that he knew what Mother's ship was called. What Jacob saw mostly were birds, such as gulls and pelicans, flying around that mid-bay island — the barren one called Alcatraces — which I had observed when we first arrived.

Jacob became increasingly distressed and anxious when Mother did not come. I admit I began to think he was right, that something bad was going to happen — not to Mother, but to him.

I would retreat behind my privacy curtain, but from his side of the tent, Jacob blathered on about his troubles and his worries. How many times did I hear him say, "Tory, if something happened to you, what would happen to me?"

Be assured, I followed Father's orders: I took care of my brother. I cooked our food — mostly beef on an open fire, which was dangerous. Though I disliked our tent, I had no desire to burn it down.

That said, our tent was a difficult place in which to live.

Always damp, the floor often got muddy. When the winds blew, we had to keep it from flying away.

Now and again I washed Jacob's clothes and mine. I kept the tent somewhat orderly. But for the most part, I worked, earning enough to buy drinking water along with food, all of which kept getting more and more expensive. Beef was cheap since it came from inland cattle ranches. But how many tough steaks can you eat?

With so much rain—the worst rain *ever*, people said— the tent reeked of mold. We woke to dank mornings. Muddy paths—those so-called streets—surrounded us and became thick, gluelike, and bottomless. When the rains eased, a damp chill permeated everything. When Jacob complained, I reminded him that in Rhode Island winters were raw and snowy. In San Francisco, it just rained or else winds blew dust all over.

There were also gray fogs, thick, wet, long lasting, which often made the city disappear. I chose to consider them mysterious.

The truth is, without anyone to scold or rule me, I was strengthened by my freedom. I came and went as I chose. I worked hard. Earned gold.

But Jacob remained a constant problem. In all the books I had read, I could recall no heroine who had been so troubled by a younger brother. It annoyed me more and more.

November came. Mother hadn't come. Father wasn't back. Jacob, not sure what to do with himself, tried to be with me *all* the time, needing me to take care of him, so that I was constantly shooing him away. As a result, he grew lonelier, unhappier about being in San Francisco.

But something else had happened, which bothered Jacob greatly. I had found a companionable friend. His name was Thaddeus Colton.

·15·

SHORTLY AFTER WE ARRIVED, I WAS AT THE COVE beach trying to improve my rowing. I had observed that bringing in ship passengers was an easy way to make money, and we had great need of it.

As I struggled to manage the two long, heavy oars, I realized a boy on the cove beach was watching me. I tried to ignore his gaze. But when I managed to get back to shore and needed to walk by him, he called out, "Having trouble rowing?"

"What business is it of yours?" I replied, thinking he was about to mock me.

"Ayuh," he said. "You're a girl."

Let it be recalled that my knowledge of boys—other than my brother—was slight. Such experience as I had—at Mrs.

Coldbrett's Academy of Dancery—was not positive. So when this boy said "You're a girl," my retort was "What if I am?"

His response was "I've got a sister who rows right enough. I'm willing to bet I can teach you."

"Why make it a bet?"

"Bets make things interesting. Besides, I'm always broke."

"Where is your sister?"

"Back east: Maine. Rowing is what we do."

"What would the bet be?"

"If I can teach you rowing, you stake me at the gambling tables."

"For how much?"

"Say . . . two dollars' worth. Gold or coin."

"What's your name?" I asked.

"Thaddeus. You can call me Thad."

"Why are you sitting here?"

"Just taking a break. I clerk at the Howard & Mellus store." He pointed. "Right there."

I considered this boy. He was tall and gawky, with unruly ginger hair, a splish-splash of freckles on his cheeks, and ears large enough that they might have served as flying jibs on a sailing ship. Fifteen years of age (as I would learn), he was rather clumsy, as if not yet accustomed to his own size. His earnest awkwardness made me smile. He rather reminded me of a scarecrow that was poorly stuffed with straw.

But since I really wanted to learn to row, I decided not to waste the opportunity.

"If you can teach me," I responded, "I'll stake you."

So it was that Thad instructed me and did so with some impatience—"No, hold your hands this way, not that." But while he could be critical, there was no condescension.

When he reminded me of the bet that he could teach me to row—which assuredly he had won—I gave him two dollars in gold grains. He went promptly to the gaming tables and lost it. I watched him do so.

He may have lost the gold, but he'd won my friendship. Whenever I'd see him at the cove, he'd offer more lessons. But he never asked for money again.

I also learned more about Thad.

His mother and sister had yet to arrive from back east. His father was a printer for the city newspaper, the *Alta California.*

Thad was not one to often smile or frown but maintained an amiable face with a mirror-smooth calmness. He spoke little, but when he did, it was with purpose. He was near my age, and I liked him because when I talked, he was willing to listen. In my life's experience, not many boys cared about what I had to say.

He, I think, enjoyed my chatter. I appreciated his calm, a kind of easy counterweight. To my exuberance, he had composure. In boat terms, that gave ballast to us both and kept our ship of friendship on an even keel.

As I learned, Thad was far from perfect. While happily he did not drink, he, like most everyone else in San Francisco, was fascinated by gambling.

He loved to wander about the gambling halls—the Mercury saloon, being nearest his work, was his favorite. Once there, he would gaze upon the thousands of dollars' worth of stacked coins and heaped gold grains. By then I had learned that his family had been quite poor in Maine. His father's coming to California—much as with my father—was an act of desperation. Thad once told me the piles of San Francisco money and gold were the nearest sight of Paradise he might ever get.

Thad would take his weekly wages and play the most popular games, faro and monte. These were card games of chance and seemed to require less skill than guesswork, which is to say luck. They were fast games, and money came and went rapidly. Sometimes Thad won, once as much as a hundred dollars. More often he would lose. It was when he played that he showed the most emotion. I came to see he loved the elation of taking risks. At times, I even felt obliged to trail after him, to make sure he did not throw away all his wages.

"It's a waste of money," I kept telling him.

"Taking chances," he returned, "adds excitement. And I just might win big."

Spending more time with Thad meant I spent less time with Jacob, which caused my brother to become unhappy about this friendship.

I explained to Jacob that Thaddeus was *not* my sweetheart. "There are few girls here," I said. "And they are too snobbish to be friends with me, dismayed by my muddy boots and hard work. Thad accepts who I am."

"I don't like him," said Jacob.

"Why?"

"Always going to the Mercury to gamble."

"Not that much, and I keep him from doing more."

Jacob, who could always find something to worry about, said, "What's going to happen if Thad gets hold of the money Father left us and gambles it away?"

"I won't let it happen," I insisted.

"But what if he does?"

"Jacob," I repeated with some anger, "it won't happen!"

Then came Monday, November 26, 1849. Rain had fallen for *five* straight days. When it finally paused, the mud was, in places, *four* feet deep. On California Street, a mule had tripped and drowned in the mire.

That early evening, Jacob was sitting outside our tent,

staring out over the bay. He was whistling a sad melody over and over again, while continually toying with that election token Father had given him. It was damp and chilly. The rain was pattering down, like the *tip-tapping* of nervous fingers.

Having something to tell him, I sat down next to him. "What's that song you are whistling?"

"It's called 'I Often Think of Writing Home.'" He turned the token over a few times. "I heard some miners singing it at the post office."

"It's a sad song," I said.

After being quiet for a while, he said, "Look at all those ships." He was gazing down at Rotten Row. "There must be *five hundred* of them now. Just sitting there. Like me. A couple are about to go east. Wish I was going."

Having learned only to listen when he complained this way, I said nothing.

He went on. "I heard ship captains are offering tons of money to hire on sailors so they can sail back east. Except no one wants to go. Some captains are even going to *crimp* for crews."

I asked, "What's *crimp* mean?"

"Captains who kidnap people to get sailors. Least I'd go somewhere."

"Jacob," I cried with exasperation, "no one is going to kidnap you."

"See that ship?" He pointed to a two-masted ship, the kind called a brig. "She's the *Yankee Sword*. Going to sail for Panama in a few days. Some kid told me the captain is looking for a cabin boy.

"I was thinking," he went on, "I should sign up. Get away from here and make some money doing it. When I get back, Mother might be here. Or Father."

"They'll never hire on a boy like you," I told him.

"Might," he said almost wistfully.

I thought, *I wish you would go*, but, instantly ashamed of myself, I said, "I promise: Father and Mother will get here soon. Father said December first. That's in five days."

"What if he doesn't come?" Jacob said mournfully.

I wasn't going to say that I could hardly wait for Father to return so that I'd no longer have the care of him.

Jacob was silent for a while before bursting out, "Tory, what if they don't *ever* come?" It was his old unhappy refrain. He reached for his hat and touched his good-luck pelican feather, which he had kept all this time.

"You're feeling bad tonight, aren't you?" I said.

"'Bout as hollow as a barrel of air. And I hate the rain."

"It'll stop."

"Yeah, but it'll start again. Always does."

After a moment, I said, "Thad and I are going to a dance tonight. You might come."

"How you going to dance in all this mud?"

I smiled. "By lifting my feet high."

He didn't laugh and declined my invitation. I had never seen such despondency in him. *Please, Father,* I thought, *come home. You've just five more days.*

I didn't press Jacob to come to the dance. Looking forward to the evening's frolic, I had no need of an unhappy younger brother stepping on my heels. The truth is, I was glad I was getting away from him.

·16·

I FETCHED UP A DRESS, MADE SURE IT WAS MOSTLY clean, and for the first time in many a day, put it on. I even scrubbed my face and brushed out my hair. I had to smile. I had forgotten what a pleasure it was to dress as a young lady.

When Thad came down the hill to our tent, he looked at me and with surprise in his voice said, "You look real pretty."

I truly believe I blushed.

The dance was held at the El Dorado Hotel. I beg you to recall my Providence dance lessons and all the rules of conduct there. This San Francisco dance was altogether different.

When Thad and I got there, the gambling tables had been pushed to one side. A fiddler and a banjo player were seated on the bar playing music, pausing only now and then to dive, like horses into their feeder bags, into buckets of drink.

"What kind of music is that?" I asked Thad.

"The polka. All the rage."

It seemed wild: great wide steps, with much whirling about, all at a rapid rate. Many people were cavorting, but since there were not many women (or girls) in San Francisco, most of the men were dancing with *men*. Nor were these men dressed in fashion as in Providence, but in their regular miner's garb. I would like to say that at least they were clean. Not so. As for noise, the carrying-on brought nothing but constant caterwauling—and no cats in sight. Rather continual hooting, hollering, and shouting, sometimes screams of elation as well. As for drinking: bottles, jugs, and barrels, constantly lifted and imbibed. Not tea, either, but not by me or Thad.

No sooner did I appear at the dance room's threshold than I was truly rushed. No dance cards here. It seemed as if three-quarters of the men asked me to dance. To my relief, Thad held them off, at least at first, while he commenced to teach me how to do that wild polka.

As for the polka, it was a dance designed for Thad's long legs, sharp elbows and knees. It was as if he came to a new life as a whirligig. As he spun me about, I became breathless, altogether hiddy-giddy. Yet the look on Thad's face was, as always, perfectly calm.

"Can't you ever smile some?"

"Thought I was," he declared. I truly believe he didn't know how.

While I danced at least thirty times with Thad, I also danced with thirty other men, who, let it be said, treated me with great respect.

All in all, nothing, *nothing* like Mrs. Coldbrett's Academy of Dancery. It was a riot set to music, though I could barely hear the tunes.

I loved it.

In my exuberance after the dance, as Thad and I walked back to my tent, we made plans that, since he had the next day off, we'd go down-bay in the morning and do some fishing and crabbing. Without much eagerness, I added, "I suppose I should ask Jacob."

"Do you have to?" said Thad.

"Think so," I returned, but I was annoyed; with Thad or Jacob, I cannot exactly say.

When I got back to the tent, exhausted but happy, I stepped right behind my curtain, glad Jacob was asleep so neither of us was obliged to talk. In any case, I wished to recall the evening alone. Once on my bed, I believe I redanced every dance. How wonderful to rollick.

• • •

In the morning, I got up early, reclaimed my miner's garb, bent over Jacob, and told him where Thad and I were heading. "Want to come?"

"No," he said, rolling away from me.

He was being, as usual, bad-tempered, making it clear he wished to have nothing to do with Thad. I, still full of my elation from the night before, thought, *Why should I let Jacob diminish my joy?*

I made one of my quick resolutions: I had done my duty. Let him sleep.

Shortly thereafter, Thad arrived at our tent. It being yet partly dark, he had brought his oil-lit lantern.

We went down to the cove.

After selecting a boat which had oars, Thad and I headed down-bay.

I don't know how many miles we both rowed, or how long it took, but we caught four salmon and fetched up a basket of crabs. With no rain or fog and a warm sun, it proved an altogether charming day. How blessed is blue sky.

Let it be said I was quite aware that I could never have spent such a time back east. A frothy dance. A morning float down the calm bay. Fishing. Crabbing. With a boy who was a friend. Next day, I'd work with Mr. Lyall, a carpenter, and make money, since he was constantly building houses. How fine it all was. I felt as if I were no longer the person I had been in Providence. I had achieved all the independence I could ever want. My spirits were so elevated, I raised my arms high and called out, "I love San Francisco!"

"Ayuh," said Thad, his Maine way of saying *yes.*

All the same, I felt obliged to return to Jacob. "We should get back," I said.

But no sooner did we start than what did I do? Rowing hurriedly, I snagged an oar on a rock so that it snapped in two.

Thad jumped into the water and, being a good swimmer, retrieved the lost half, then climbed back into our boat, dripping wet.

I used my knife (the one Father had given me) and tried to whittle a new blade from the stump of the remaining broken oar.

"Let me do that," said Thad.

Frustrated, I gave the knife over, and though it was sharp, his efforts were no better than mine. So it was that we had to work our way to town with but one full oar, paddling the boat like a canoe. At times the tide and currents ran against us. Getting back to the cove seemed to take as long as sailing to California from back east.

It must have been close to midnight, then, when Thad and I, holding our catch in our hands, trudged uphill to my tent. Thad's lantern had long expired. There was just enough moonlight to make our way.

Thad set down the basket of crabs he had been carrying. I flipped the tent flap open and poked my head into the deeper darkness.

"Jacob," I called. "Sorry I'm so late. Our oar broke. We had to paddle home. But look: we caught some fish and crabs. Jacob?"

There being no response, I looked closer. Jacob was *not* in his bed.

·17·

I BACKED OUT OF THE TENT. "JACOB'S NOT HERE."

"You sure?" Thad poked his head in, only to retreat. "Nope," he said. "Not here."

Doubting myself, I looked a second time. Jacob was not there.

"Where do you think he went?" Thad asked.

"Must have got tired waiting for me and went to a friend."

Though I said that, I knew my brother had few friends and those he had were not people I knew. I did look up and down the hill, but as far as I could see, the dreary, muddy street-paths were desolate. Nearby tents were dark. A tent farther off, lit from the inside, glowed. But I didn't think Jacob, being shy, was likely to seek refuge with strangers. I felt uneasy.

Thad said, "Want to find him?"

Across the way, Señor Rosales's restaurant, where Jacob often was, stood closed down for the night. Since the café had no door, I crossed over and peeked inside. Señor Rosales was asleep in his coffin. There was no sign of Jacob.

"He'll be back," I said, feeling more annoyed than anything.

Thad said, "Got to go. My old man will be fretting. I'd bet you're right: he'll show up in the morning."

I didn't take the bet, but I gave Thad two fish. "Your share. And take the crabs. Jacob doesn't like them."

Thad pushed his fingers through the salmon gills and hefted the basket. "Guess I need my lantern," he said.

I hung it over his free fingers. "Sorry about that oar."

"Nothing," he said, then stepped away through the mud. As he went he lifted the fish and let their tails wave goodbye. "Got work tomorrow," he called.

"Me too," I called back. "But we need to replace that oar. When I get some time, I'll come down to your store and get one." I watched him move uphill and soon disappear.

I stood before the tent, thinking about Jacob, where he might be. Downhill, I saw that Portsmouth Square, the center of the city, was yet abloom with lights along with shouts of men, and music too. Since my brother had no affection for gambling or drinking I was sure he had not gone to such places. Besides, at that late hour, I didn't think it was safe for me to go there alone.

All this meant I had no idea—and, let it be said, no great desire—to seek Jacob out. All the same, I kept wondering, *Where is he?*

Standing in the darkness, the chill wind rising, I turned back to the tent and stared into it. This was something that Jacob had never done before. Of course, I had to acknowledge, I'd never come back so late, either. I recalled that though I had told him where I was going that morning, he had been sleepy and might not have heard. A twinge of self-blame reminded me I had not made certain he'd heard me.

Leaving the remaining fish by the entryway, I went into our tent. On hands and knees—I couldn't see a thing— I felt on the left side of the dirt floor for my sleeping space. When I found it, I untied my money belt from around my waist, checked to make sure I had my knife, and poked all under my bed.

I lay down and drew Mother's shawl up to my chin. It being chilly, I was happy to be covered. As I listened to the wind luffing our tent cloth, I hoped that Jacob—wherever he might be—was warm.

For a while, I thought about my day with Thad. I had so enjoyed it, not the least because I was free of clinging Jacob. That thought brought me to remember his idle chatter about seeking employment on a departing ship. Could he have done that?

No, not in a million years.

Then, where is he?

I told myself he was not a baby and in all likelihood, I'd see him in the morning, grumbling as ever. I even told myself that he might well have chosen to be away from the tent to vex me, to make me worry about him.

So it was that I pushed aside my feelings of uneasiness and rolled over to my right, sleeping side. A few moments later, rain began to splatter hard against the tent cloth. Its steady beat lulled me.

As I began to drift off, Father's words came into my head: "I'm depending on you to take care of the boy. Mother is depending on it. Is that clearly understood?"

My last waking thought was: *Nothing has happened to Jacob. Nothing.* That comforting idea eased me into sleep.

·18·

IN THE MORNING I LAY ABED, LISTENING TO THE soft, steady patter of rain upon our tent. The sound reminded me that the weather was *outside*. I was within, dry and warm: a sweet and soothing feeling.

I'd been so tired the night before that I'd fallen asleep in my clothing. A night of dancing followed by a day of hard rowing *will* cause fatigue. That led me to think, with more pleasure, about the day before. I recalled too that Mother must surely come soon. And Father was due in a few days. They would, I hoped, be proud of me for having managed myself and Jacob so well.

All this put me in such good spirits that I called out a "Good morning!" to Jacob but received no reply. Belatedly, I remembered that when I returned late the night before, he was not in his bed.

I lay there, choosing to believe his absence was his way of showing resentment for my spending the day with Thad. Moments later, I told myself surely by this time he would have come back. I decided he was most likely with Señor Rosales.

I also considered the possibility that he had gone to Portsmouth Square to look for gold. The low angle of the sun — if there was sun — sparked lost grains. Mornings were the best time to look since drunken men stumbled about late at night. If I found Jacob there, I knew he'd tease me: he was working when I slept. That reminded me I'd promised Mr. Lyall, the carpenter, that I'd work with him that day.

I drew out my money belt from under my bed, checked for my money and knife, fastened it around my waist, and told myself that I needed to make sure Jacob was all right before I set off for work.

I stuck my head out of our tent. It was still drizzling, and too overcast to establish the time. Across the way, despite the inclement weather, the San Francisco Café Restaurant was open for business, with a few customers waiting in line to be served. As always, Señor Rosales was at his stove, cooking, smoke rising up through his tin chimney.

"Buenos días, Señor Rosales," I called as I walked over. It was clear right away that Jacob was not there. I told the señor what happened to Thad and me, that when I got back Jacob was gone. "Have you seen him?"

"Lo siento — sorry to hear what happened, corderita," said Señor Rosales. "All I can tell you is your hermano — your brother — was worried about you."

"He's always worried," I said.

"True. But this time, más. To tell you my thoughts, señorita, I think el se siente solo. He was feeling lonely. More than usual. It's what I told your father. Not wise to leave him solo — alone."

"I told Jacob he could come with us," I said, somewhat uncomfortable, aware that I had not truly encouraged him to come down the bay.

"Can I give you some breakfast?" Señor Rosales offered me a piece of beef, which I quickly ate.

"I have to go to work," I announced. "If you see Jacob, por favor, señor, tell him I'm working with Mr. Lyall. Ask him to come to me."

"Absolutamente, corderita."

I stood before our tent, not sure what to do: work or find Jacob. A younger brother who hampers one's life is most irritating. All the same, I felt I should locate him, tell him where I'd be, that we should have dinner together — my way of absolving myself for slighting him the day before.

I hurried over to Portsmouth Square, but he was not on the grounds. I eyed the gambling places. Whenever I passed by the entryways of the Parker House and the El Dorado, I heard shouts, laughter, screams, and music. Often, horrid fights broke out among the men. Once, when passing a saloon, I heard pistol shots. Greatly frightened, I had watched as a dead man was borne away on an old door. Alas, such violence was common in this wild city.

Though I much doubted Jacob had gone into either place, I told myself that if I was going to solve the aggravating puzzle of his whereabouts, I should make sure.

I went into El Dorado.

Unlike the night of the dance, gambling and drinking were already going on. I was bumped, shoved, and generally stomped on by the crowd of tough, loudmouthed men and a few women.

It didn't take long to determine that Jacob wasn't there. Then I did a quick check of the post office. He was not standing in the lines waiting for mail.

I made a return trip to our tent, in hopes he had come back. He had not. Nor had Señor Rosales caught sight of him.

It was about then that I began to truly worry. It was absolutely not like Jacob to stay away for so long.

The rain had lessened and the morning fog had thinned, enough so that I could look down at the bay and Rotten Row. I saw the ship that Jacob had pointed out, the *Yankee Sword*. She was still there.

Remembering our last conversation, I wondered—could he have, in fact, signed on? No, I refused to consider such a possibility. Jacob would *never* do something that would be so unusual for him.

Seeing that new ships had arrived, I considered that he might be at the cove beach, in hopes Mother had arrived. That *would* be something he would do.

Going downhill, I passed some frame houses being built, on places which had been mud a couple of days ago. I even passed Mr. Lyall, the carpenter I'd promised to help.

"Hey, Miss Tory," he called. "You're late."

"I need to find Jacob," I called back. "Have you seen him?"

"Nope. But I can use him too."

"Soon as I find him, I'll come," I said, gave a wave, and continued on.

At the cove beach, lighters were hauling in throngs of newcomers and their baggage. Other boats were bringing men back from the diggings. The contrast was extreme: newcomers happy and excited. Returning miners emaciated, filthy, and dispirited, shivering with malarial fevers. I suddenly felt a twinge of Jacob's apprehension: What if Father did not return? What if he was ill? Injured? Had found no gold? All were real possibilities.

There was no sign of Jacob among the onlookers at the cove. Nor, for that matter, of Mother.

I did remind myself that I had an obligation to replace the oar I had broken the day before. Then it also occurred to me that perhaps Jacob, in search of me while I was looking for him, might have gone to see Thad.

I hurried over to the store where Thad clerked.

The Howard & Mellus store sold all kinds of the dry goods that miners needed, from slouch hats to shoes, picks to pans and the things ships required. The store even posted ship arrivals and departures.

As usual, it was crowded, and it was almost comical to watch the faces of newcomers when they were told the prices of the things they desired: Fifty dollars for a pickax. Forty dollars for a pound of coffee.

I found Thad at the back of the store piling up canvas trousers.

"Morning," he called when he saw me. "I put aside a new oar for that boat we used. Forty dollars. But I lost twenty-five at the tables this morning. I'll owe you. Jacob back?"

I was annoyed by his betting but, being more concerned with Jacob, I only replied to his question. "Not yet."

"You ask Señor Rosales?"

"He said Jacob was looking for me. Thad, if he comes by, tell him I'll be working with Mr. Lyall, or to go back to the tent and wait."

"Ayuh. He'll show up."

He fetched the new oar, which I signed for and brought back to the cove and left in the boat we had borrowed. Then I sat in the boat. Dejected, growing ever more concerned, I tried to think where I might look for Jacob. I needed to find him to settle myself.

Near the building where Thad worked was the Mercury saloon. The *Mercury* was one of those ships that had been left in Rotten Row. Somebody had purchased her and hauled her hulk over the Yerba Buena Cove flats. With pilings made from her masts, she was fixed against the new Central Wharf and turned into a building—a gambling saloon.

For San Francisco that was not unusual. Right across the way, another ship, the *Euphemia,* still afloat, was being turned into a new city jail. Other empty boats had become hotels, warehouses, and hospitals. One was becoming a church.

As for the landlocked *Mercury,* her bow had been sawed off and squared. Over the entryway was a sloping roof, where the name MERCURY SALOON had been painted in huge letters.

Since the saloon was right on the cove shore, miners came directly from the diggings up-bay and began to gamble with their newfound gold. Some won. Most lost, and did so quickly. As a result, the place was always full of the frenzy of hope and desperation as these men cast away what they had worked so hard to get.

The Mercury fascinated many, including Thad. Jacob knew

he liked going in. Hadn't Thad even gone in this morning? Jacob also knew I had been there any number of times, trying to get Thaddeus to leave.

It occurred to me that perhaps Jacob went to the Mercury to look for us and that someone had seen him. But with the Mercury's reputation for being one of the worst saloons, you may be sure I liked it no more than the places on Portsmouth Square.

I was reluctant to go inside.

Stop making excuses, Tory, I told myself. *You need to find Jacob.*

I went in.

·19·

T HE MERCURY WAS ALWAYS SWARMING DURING late afternoons and nights, but when I went in that morning, the crowd was sparse. Despite the early hour, the glass chandeliers were already lit. Huge wall-size mirrors were polished, there to make everything bigger, brighter. Behind drinking counters were shelves set against the walls, displaying great numbers of liquor bottles as well as glass jars full of free peppermints. The air smelled of whale oil fumes, which mingled with the odor of whiskey and stale tobacco. It made me wrinkle my nose.

It was almost impossible to believe the place had been a ship, not unlike the *Stephanie K.*, in which I had come to California. Yet its transformation was so like San Francisco.

There were multiple roulette and billiards tables, as well as gambling tables covered with green cloth, behind which — though it was just morning — sat professional gamblers. Around these men were stacks of coins and piles of gold dust, worth, Thad had told me, as much as five thousand dollars. The money was there to tempt miners to try their luck at games of chance.

During crowded times, enthusiastic men would line up three, four deep, shoving forward so they could place bets. There were just as many stumbling the other way who, having become abruptly impoverished, had faces that were maps of misery.

If I had learned anything about San Francisco, it was this: the men might have been in a fever to get gold, but they were just as feverish to wager it away.

As I stood in the middle of the long hall — the ship's hull — and observed the entire sparkly place, I saw no sign of Jacob. But I did notice that on a stage in the back, where musicians performed, a solitary Negro boy was sitting on a chair, playing a brass-keyed bugle. The melody was that sad "I Often Think of Writing Home," which I recognized as the one Jacob had been whistling. Willing to make any connection to my brother, I wandered back to the stage.

I thought the bugler somewhat the same age as I, skinny like me, with coffee-colored skin and bushy, curly hair. He wore frayed trousers and a flannel shirt somewhat large for him, the cuffs rolled back over thin wrists. Boots. Though his face was narrow, his cheeks, as he played, bulged like chicken eggs. His fingers were long and slender and moved with great assurance over the keys, bringing forth the song with a smooth, melancholy tone.

As I stood there, dressed for work, which is to say, not in my feminine attire, looking and listening to him play, I was sure he noticed me, but he didn't do or say anything.

"Good morning," I finally called.

The boy, without stopping his playing, glanced over to me and gave no more than a bob to his instrument to acknowledge my presence.

It was only when I continued to stand there that he abruptly stopped playing, lowered his bugle, and considered me with angry eyes, as if to say I was interrupting him. Though I suspected he wished I'd go away, I chose to take advantage of his pause as a chance to say something.

"Do you play in the band?" I asked.

He lifted his horn as if to say that was obvious.

"The tune you were playing, 'I Often Think of Writing Home'—my brother likes it."

His face softened a little. "OK," he said without emotion.

"My name is Victoria Blaisdell. Tory."

After a moment, he gave a nod. "Samuel Nichols. Sam."

"What part of the states do you come from?" I asked. In San Francisco, when you met people, that was the way friendly conversations most often started.

He hesitated before saying, "New York State. You?"

"Rhode Island," I said, pleased that the Yankee connection gave us something in common. "Were you playing here last night?"

His look grew wary. "What if I was?"

"It's my younger brother," I said. "Jacob. He's gone off somewhere. I don't know where, so I'm searching for him. Since he likes music—and that song you were playing was his favorite—I thought he might have been here last night and you saw him."

"Lot of people here last night. What's he look like?"

I described Jacob.

The boy was silent for a moment and then said, "Last night, a kid like that was standing right where you are, watching and listening to me play that tune. When I stopped, he went off."

Here, at last, was news. "Do you have any idea where?" I asked with eagerness.

Sam shook his head. "All I do is make music." As if to make his point, he turned from me, lifted his bugle, and began to play that melody again, "I Often Think of Writing Home." I took it to mean he was not going to say any more.

Though frustrated, I said, "Thank you," and turned away, uncertain where I should go next. All I could think to do was to go back up the hill and wait.

I had almost reached the Mercury's front doors when a man stepped in front of me, blocking my way. With his high stovepipe hat, he loomed over me. He was a tall man, his face shaped like the letter V, with a trimmed dark beard and elegant jacket with black cravat and white collar. His long nose brought to mind a blackbird or a crow. I took him to be one of the professional gamblers.

"Yes, miss, what brings you here?" he demanded as if he had the right to know.

Though I thought him ill-mannered, at least he recognized me as a girl. "Yes, sir," I said. "I'm looking for my brother."

"That a fact. What's he look like?"

I described him.

"A kid."

"Ten."

He frowned. "Little young to be here, isn't he? But nope. Can't say I ever saw him. What makes you think he *was* here?"

"That boy"—I pointed toward the back of the saloon, and Sam—"the bugler, he told me he saw him."

The man glanced toward the stage. Then he turned back to me with unfriendly eyes. "I was here all last night," he said. "And I didn't see anyone like you described. Now, you can trust me or you can trust that colored kid. Hate to tell you: he's not one for speaking the truth much. Anyway, I don't think a girl should be in here. You better move on out."

Not only were his words offensive, but the way he spoke and studied me was intimidating. I almost blurted out what I thought: "I'd trust the boy before you," but decided I had best leave. In any case, the man—whoever he was—had told me to go. "Thank you, sir," I managed to say.

The man stepped aside and allowed me to move toward the entry. I had no idea who he was, but as I walked away I belatedly realized that he had a pelican feather attached to his jacket lapel. It was just like the one Father had given Jacob.

·20·

N O SOONER DID I LEAVE THE MERCURY THAN I considered returning and asking that man about the feather. But he had made me feel uncomfortable and I took him for a bully, what some people called a ring-tailed roarer. Then—making excuses—I told myself there were a million pelican feathers around. It was simpler—easier—not to go back.

Besides, I was feeling somewhat reassured; that bugler, Sam, *had* seen Jacob in the Mercury last night. I took it to confirm that, at least, my brother had not signed on—which I had not truly thought possible—with that Panama-bound ship, the *Yankee Sword*.

Not sure what to do next, I thought the only other place worth looking for Jacob was atop Goat Hill—where he often went to watch for Mother's ship's arrival. But heavy rain had recommenced, and I could not imagine him sitting midst that soak. In any case, I decided to go back to the tent, in hopes he'd returned.

Struggling to stay free of mud, crowds, and scattered rubbish, I hurried uphill toward home, all the while telling myself that to worry was ridiculous. And yet I did worry. For let it be admitted: it was my growing sense that I had failed in my responsibilities toward Jacob that made me uneasy. It was as if I, in some fashion, had caused his wandering off. I had spent a day away from him and come back from my trip down-bay with Thad late. Yet, I hastily reminded myself, the cause was the broken oar, not me. Still, when something bad happens and you think it might be your fault, it always seems worse.

By the time I reached our tent, I had built up hopeful expectations that Jacob would be there. A quick look inside told me he had not returned.

Dispirited, troubled anew, I sat on one of our beds. The more I thought about it, the more upset I became. It may have been bothersome to always look after Jacob, but it was quite another to have him disappear. I was—I reminded myself—in charge of him. Yes, a sibling can be annoying, but there is no one you love more.

To ease my tension, I told myself this was just a small

mystery, a mystery called *Where was Jacob?* Did I not like enigmas, the unknown? Was not the sky suitably gray and low? Like a description in a book, it fit the moment. That is to say, I told myself that this would be a modest puzzle: I should embrace it. Solve it quickly.

"Jacob," I said aloud, "please come back!"

I went across to the café.

"Do you find Jacob, corderita?" Señor Rosales called out as soon as he saw me.

Two men dressed like miners were standing at his wood-plank counter, eating.

I shook my head. "Have you seen him?"

"No lo he visto. I haven't seen him," he said. "Can I offer you some comida—food—now?"

"Gracias."

I stood at the serving counter as he gave me a cup of coffee and a slab of beef. I reached into my money belt.

He held up his palm. "Más tarde. Later, corderita. When you find Jacob."

"Who's Jacob?" asked one of the men who had been eating. In San Francisco strangers talked to strangers all the time.

"My younger brother," I said.

"Where's he at?"

"I don't know."

"Probably went to the diggings," said the man as he put a

pinch of gold grains into Señor Rosales's outstretched hand to pay for his meal.

"He's too young," I said. But I had not thought it before: perhaps he had gone off to find Father. It was something I could almost see him, out of frustration, attempting.

"Never too young to get rich," said the man. "I heard tell yesterday of a nine-year-old boy digging alongside his old man up on the San Joaquin River. Pulled up a two-thousand-dollar nugget."

As the miners headed out, one of them paused and looked hard at me. "Excuse me, you a boy or a girl?"

"A girl," I said, holding my head high.

"Nice to see one," he said, touching his hat with civility. "Not all that many around here." He started to leave, hesitated, and looked back. "Married, ma'am?" he said.

"No wish to be," I said, giving the answer I had learned to use.

"Hope you don't mind me asking," said the miner with a shy smile. Then he touched his hat in politeness again and left.

Señor Rosales stood behind his counter, arms folded over his chest. "You are distressed, corderita, aren't you?"

"Jacob has never gone like this," I answered.

"No idea where he would go?"

"He talked of shipping out."

"Jacob? Nunca. Never."

"Or maybe he did go off to find Father."

Señor Rosales shook his head. "Not without telling you."

"At the Mercury, there was a musician, a boy. From what he told me, Jacob had been listening to the music there last night. He must have been there looking for me."

"Well, then, ask that niño."

"I did. He said he had no idea where Jacob went."

"Preguntale otra vez. Perhaps he'll remember something else. People do."

"I suppose," I admitted.

When I finished eating, I went back to our tent and decided to wait until Jacob returned.

I took off my hat and smoothed back my hair, feeling how quickly it had become dirty again. Telling myself I should buy some soap at Thad's store, I pulled my hair around, braided it anew, and tried to be patient.

Perhaps Señor Rosales was right: I should speak to that bugler boy again. Perhaps he had remembered something. *Any* hint as to where Jacob had gone would ease my worry. Then I reminded myself: Father was due back in three days. What if, by then, I could not find Jacob? The thought gave me a jolt of panic.

Ignoring the rain and mud, I headed back toward the Mercury.

·21·

THE SALOON WAS MUCH MORE CROWDED THAN before, the noise already full-mouthed. At the entryway, I looked first for that not-so-nice man, the one with the pelican feather on his coat lapel. Relieved not to see him, I went to the stage at the back of the hall, hoping the Negro boy was there. When I saw he wasn't, my heart seemed to drop. The only one on the low stage was an old white man, sweeping. His full gray beard was unkempt, his head bald, his mouth collapsed, his eyes bleary red. With his ragged clothing, I judged him to be a failed miner. Such men were all over town.

Not knowing what else to do, I stood waiting on him, but he paid no attention to me. Instead, he worked his broom in slow, ceaseless circles, now and again pausing to throw out a clogged cough.

"Sir," I called at last, "can you tell me where the musicians are?"

The old man paused in his work and gazed at me as though waking from a dream. "Musicians?" he asked, and coughed as if his throat were full of phlegm.

I said, "There was a black boy here, a bugler. He told me his name was Samuel. Sam."

The old man stared at me, but not as if he were seeing. He let forth a few more coughs, which shook his whole body. When he stopped, he drew his trembling hand over his mouth and wiped a gob of whatever it was he had spit up and smeared it on his trousers.

"Sir," I prompted, "I need to speak to that boy."

"One of the musicians?" he said, as much to himself as me. "The colored kid? Don't know much 'bout him, save him and his father live over in Happy Valley. Used to have an older brother. Don't know what happened to him, either." He coughed, spat, turned away, and resumed his slow sweeping. It had hardly been a conversation, but when he turned his back on me, I knew it was over.

"Thank you," I muttered, and headed for the doors, making my way through the unruly gamblers. I again looked for the man I didn't like but caught no sight of him. Dejected, I passed through the entryway. But once outside, it was clear that if I wished to speak to that bugler, I must go find him in Happy Valley.

Happy Valley was a small area south of what people were calling Market Street, situated at the southern end of Yerba Buena Cove, near a place called Rincon Point. No ships came there, not even the abandoned ones. I suppose the name—Happy Valley—was meant as a jest because the men with whom I had worked had taken pains to tell me there was no valley and little happiness there, that it was not a place to picnic or sniff the air. Rather, it was an area full of sludge, sewage, and gross mud. That if one desired to define the word *dreadful* or *nasty* you might as well describe Happy Valley.

Thad had spoken about it too, saying that Happy Valley was the most crowded, poorest part of the city. Crowded, he said, because people could live there without paying rent—squatters. Most of all, it was the section of the city where discarded people and things were shunted. The people living there, he said, had had the worst kind of luck, were sick, or poor. More often than not, they were a mix of all three. Once you lived there, he said, you tended to remain as if stuck in its mud. Thad also claimed that people who had committed crimes often took up residence there, since it was common knowledge that the city's new, small police force refused to venture into the area.

In other words, all agreed that Happy Valley was the last place I should visit. But though it might be the worst of San

Francisco, if I wanted to speak to the boy Sam, that's where I had to go.

So it was that not long after I left the Mercury, I stood at the unhappy neighborhood's edge, where I could see for myself much of what I had been told. The people I saw walking about appeared forsaken. Nary a cheerful face. Nor did I see any women. Or girls. As I remained there, seeking the courage to go forward, I remembered Father saying when he left, "Try and act a little ladylike."

No, going into Happy Valley was hardly ladylike. It might, I had been warned, even be perilous. Yet Father had also told me that I must be responsible for my brother. I couldn't have it both ways. In any case my agitation had only grown. I *had* to find Jacob. Of course, there was nothing to suggest that the bugle boy—if I could even find him—knew anything more than he had already told me.

But as Señor Rosales had suggested, Sam might have remembered *something* after I left. I, therefore, felt obliged to speak to him, the last to have seen Jacob, thus being the only thread I could clutch, my tiny clue as to my brother's whereabouts. Except, as I stood there—before Happy Valley— I didn't even know how to start looking for him.

Then I heard a slow, sad weep of music which drifted over the dilapidated dwellings clear and clean. I knew it right away, the song I'd heard the bugle boy play: "I Often Think of Writing Home."

I told myself that it had to be Sam.

Hoping the music would continue so I could follow it to the source, I reminded myself I must be careful not to get lost. From my money belt, I wiggled out my knife and kept it hidden in my hand. Only then did I step forward.

You might think that trying to trace the source of the music would be easy. But there was no order to the place. Pathways were never straight. The people living there had used anything and everything that might give shelter and set it up at utter random: tents, slapdash shacks, lopsided packing-box homes, a cloth tied to four (or two) poles, sheets of old sail-cloth used for making tents or spread upon the ground, under which people lay.

As I walked, moving along the winding, pinching pathways that lay between tents, shacks, and sleeping spots, the music stopped or became soft. Which meant I too had to stop and pray it might resume. Each time it halted, I'd whisper, as if to that boy Samuel, "Keep playing. Keep playing."

As I continued on, men appeared from what seemed to be nowhere. Seeing me, they stopped, their looks poking at me, their raw gazes rude and rough, sometimes altogether alarming, as if daring me to go forward. At such moments, I felt the need to retreat and find another route. Never had I been so glad I was not in young woman's dress.

I kept wandering, constantly checking behind me in hopes I'd remember a way out. I was not sure I could. Fortunately, the music repeated itself, over and over again. Oh, how sad it sounded. Yet, oddly, it gave me hope.

At length, the music guided me to a tent, a tent made of blue cloth, square and somewhat larger than ours. It was wedged between other tents, so there was not much space around it.

With my knife concealed in hand, I stood and listened to the music. Though relieved I'd found where I thought the boy Samuel lived, I dithered, reminding myself that he might not know anything more about Jacob. Nor had he been friendly. I had no idea what he, a colored boy, might think of me, a white girl. He might resent my coming. I further admit, by then I was already wondering how I was ever going to find my way out of Happy Valley.

Telling myself I had come this far, that I had to at least *try* to speak to the boy, I put my knife away, stood before the tent opening, and called, "Samuel Nichols. Samuel. Sam!"

Instantly the music stopped.

·22·

THERE WAS NO REPLY TO MY CALL.

"Hello!" I tried again. "Is Samuel there? May I speak to him, *please*? It's me, Victoria Blaisdell. Tory."

When there was still no response, I stepped back, trying to think what I should do. *He won't come,* I told myself. *He doesn't want to speak to me.* I was about to leave when someone poked his head out of the tent.

It wasn't Sam but an older Negro man, with touches of white in his hair. His dark, wrinkled face made me think he was old enough to be the boy's grandfather. His look was solemn, suggesting he was not pleased to see me. For a long moment, he studied me as if trying to read me. Then he said, "What do you want, miss?"

"Please, sir. I'm looking for a boy named Samuel," I said, wishing to be as polite as I could.

"Why?" he demanded.

"I'm trying to find my brother. He's disappeared."

Alarm filled the man's face. "Are you saying that Samuel had something to do with your brother going missing?"

"Oh, no, sir. I'm just looking for help finding him."

"What's Samuel got to do with it?"

"He's the last person I know to have seen him."

The man continued to consider me with distrustful eyes. "Where," he said, "was that?"

"Last night. At the Mercury."

"Was he gambling?"

"Oh, no, sir. He's only ten years old."

"Ten! What was he doing in the Mercury? At night?"

"I think he was looking for me."

"Where were *you*?" His tone was severe.

"I was fishing down-bay. With a friend. Only I was stuck there. When I finally got back, my brother was gone. I don't know where. I've been looking for him."

"What's your brother's name?"

"Jacob. I spoke to Samuel this morning. He told me that he saw Jacob last night listening to him play at the Mercury."

"I'm Samuel's father. Mr. Nichols. How'd you know Sam lived here?"

"An old man at the Mercury told me. When I got here, I heard Sam playing that song, 'I Often Think of Writing Home.' I followed it."

"How old are you?"

"Fourteen, sir."

"Where are your parents?"

"My father is at the diggings. My mother hasn't come out yet."

"You telling me you and your brother are here in this city *alone*?"

"Yes, sir."

"And you said your name is . . . Victoria?"

"Yes, sir."

"A girl, right?"

I nodded.

Mr. Nichols frowned, and his eyes never stopped appraising me. "I need to get this right: You and your brother are in San Francisco *alone*. Now he's missing, but you're *not* blaming Samuel?"

"Oh, no, sir. I just need help finding him."

As if trying to make up his mind, Samuel's father continued looking at me. At last, he said, "All right. You can step in. For a minute."

With one hand, he held the tent flap wide. With the

other, he made a beckoning gesture. It was not a welcome but permission.

I hesitated for a half second, but then I said, "Thank you, sir," and went in.

The dim tent was neater than Jacob and I kept ours. Three beds were laid out side by side. Two boxes stood in the back area. Sitting on one of the beds was Sam, the key bugle on his lap. When he glanced up at me, his face showed not the slightest recognition. All the same, I was sure he must have recognized me and heard the conversation.

"Do you know this girl?" his father said to him. His eyes were severe but, I thought, protective.

Sam considered me for a brief moment. "This morning," he said to his father, not to me, "when I was practicing at the Mercury, she was asking about her brother being there."

"I think Jacob was looking for me," I interjected.

Still speaking to his father, Sam said, "I told her I don't know anything about him."

"Did he tell you that?" Mr. Nichols demanded of me.

"Yes, sir."

"Then what else do you want?" There was displeasure in his voice.

"Please, sir," I said, speaking fast because I was nervous, "I was hoping Samuel might have remembered *something* that could help me. I have to find my brother. And another thing: Jacob had a pelican feather in his hat. Our father gave it to him before he went to the mines. When I was in the Mercury this morning, after I spoke to you"—I nodded to Sam—"a man demanded to know what I was doing there. When I told him, he said Jacob hadn't been in the Mercury. Told me to leave. But the thing is, he had a feather on his coat—a pelican feather— just like Jacob had."

As I spoke, Mr. Nichols's face filled with unease. "What man was that?"

"Tall, narrow face, long nose. Trimmed beard. Black cravat and high hat."

Sam and his father exchanged looks of alarm. Their silent exchange made me think they knew the person I was talking about. Even so, Mr. Nichols said, "We know nothing about that man."

I waited for them to say more. When they didn't, though I was disappointed, there was nothing for me to do but say "Thank you" and start to leave.

"Hold on," called Mr. Nichols.

I stopped.

"What's your name again?"

"Victoria, sir. Victoria Blaisdell. You can call me Tory."

"OK, Miss Tory. Can you find your way out of here? It can be a fuddle."

"I . . . hope I can."

Mr. Nichols made a gesture to Samuel. "You better show her the way."

Sam looked at his father with, I thought, a question in his eyes. I think I saw his father give a tiny shake of his head. A "no." I had no idea what it meant.

Regardless, Sam put his bugle down on the bed, stood up, and said to me, "Come on."

I went out of the tent first. Sam followed. I kept thinking, *What did that no mean?*

·23·

WITHOUT SAYING A WORD, SAM PASSED ME AND, not so much as looking around, started walking fast. I had no choice but to trail after, hurrying to keep up. As I looked at him, I could see how tense his body was. It seemed as if he wanted to get away from something. Perhaps it was me. Was he angry?

He picked his way through the disorder of tents and shacks as if leading me through a maze. Hoping I could get him to speak, I called out, "Why do you keep playing that song, 'I Often Think of Writing Home'?"

"Wish I *were* home," he snapped without looking around.

He continued on at the same pace until he stopped abruptly and turned around. I could see his eyes shifting as if checking to see if we were alone. Apparently satisfied that we were, he said, "That man you were asking about, the one who said he hadn't seen your brother, his name is Kassel. Mr. John Kassel."

"Why didn't you say so before?"

"My father's fearful of him. And I'm not going to pretend I'm not too."

"Fearful? But . . . why? Who is he?"

"Mr. Kassel runs the Mercury. Our boss. If we say anything bad about him and he hears about it, no telling what he'll do. A lot of the people around here don't like us."

"I don't understand."

Momentarily, his eyes shifted away from me, then he looked right at me. "I'm guessing you know that some people don't like Negroes." I wanted to say that wasn't me, but his severe tone and bluntness tied my tongue. I stared at him, hoping to hear more.

"I told you this morning," he went on, "we're from New York State. Town of Sag Harbor. Nothing like San Francisco. Small whaling town. There's no slavery in New York. We're free men. My brother and I and other kids went to school, church. Best of all, we'd roam around, swim, fish. Just live.

"Then my father wanted to try for the gold here. Thought he could get rich."

"Like my father," I said.

"There was a converted whaling ship," continued Sam.

"The *General Parsons,* coming out from Sag Harbor. One of the early ones. I'd already sailed on her. We hired on as shipmen and musicians. Soon as we got here—this past July—the whole crew rushed to the diggings. We went too. But we were run out. Not just us. Mexicans. People from Chile. We had to come back to town. With almost no money.

"Nothing we could do," Sam went on, "but stay here, work as musicians until we save enough money to buy our way back to New York—but direct to New York, see?—safe and sure.

"No slavery in California, but the problem is, we can't go back east just anywhere. Has to be New York. Or Massachusetts. Free states. If we go to the Carolinas, states like that, they might turn us into slaves."

I nodded, even as I tried to make sense of it all.

"Which is why we work for that Mr. Kassel. It's what we *have* to do to make money. Can you understand all that?"

"I think so," I said, unnerved by his tale. Then I found the voice to say, "I'm sorry for your troubles." The words sounded weak to my own ears.

I stood there, feeling stupid, not knowing what else to say, all too aware that Sam was watching me closely. But then I said, "Do you think this Mr. Kassel knows something about my brother?"

"No idea. But I'd trust him like I'd trust a snake with fangs at both ends. Let me tell you something, girl." He paused as if needing to decide to go on. "This morning," he continued, "after you left, Kassel came back and asked me if I'd spoken to a white girl. Said I wasn't allowed to do that."

"He did?"

"I knew it was you he was talking about. But no telling what Kassel might do, so I lied. Said I hadn't. I hope you can understand that. Just trying to protect ourselves. Now I've spoken too much. My father didn't want me to say anything."

"Why?"

"I just told you," he said, this time with anger, then he turned about and said, "Let's go," and once more he began to lead the way.

But he didn't take five steps when he once again stopped and faced me. "I'm guessing you have no idea what a . . . a crimp is, do you?"

I remembered that Jacob had used that word: something about kidnapping. Not being sure, I shook my head.

"All these ships that come here, like ours, like the *General Parsons,* soon as they arrive, they lose their crews. Head for the gold. So the ships can't go anywhere."

Remembering what had happened when the *Stephanie K.* reached San Francisco and the whole crew went off, I said, "Rotten Row."

"Exactly. Rotten Row. Ships just sitting in the cove. Or, like the *Mercury,* turned into a saloon. Which means captains get desperate for sailors so they can sail back home. Get frantic enough, they come to Kassel. He's a crimp. He feeds drink or drugs to people who are in the Mercury. When they pass out, Kassel sells them to the captains for crew. Gets good money for each one he hands over. The Mercury being right on the water, it's easy to deliver them. When they wake up, they're at sea."

"Drugs them!" I cried, my heart lurching. "Sells them?"

"You never heard it from me."

"But . . . but that's . . . slavery."

"Don't even *try* to tell me anything about slavery. White folks think slavery is just about black people. Don't you believe it.

"But I'll tell *you* something, Miss Tory. My father and I, we never eat or drink anything in the Mercury. Too risky. That Mr. Kassel, he suits up fine, but he's as savage as a meat ax. He'd mince his mother for money. That's why my father told me to say nothing to you. Not to protect you, but us. Now that you know, do us a big favor: keep away."

Shocked, I just stood there.

Sam, if he noticed my reaction, said nothing, only turned about and started walking again. I hurried after him.

But once again, he stopped. "I'll tell you another thing," he said. "If Kassel took your brother, that means it's for a ship that's sailing soon."

"Soon?" I cried. "How soon?"

"No idea. Quick."

"Why?"

"Because the sooner that crimped person gets sailed off, the better. Makes sense, doesn't it? He's gone. No body. No crime. Vanished. You won't see him again. Ever. That's the way Kassel works."

I think I may have actually gulped. "Are you saying Jacob might . . . already be gone?"

Not answering, Sam resumed walking, as if trying to get away from what he had already revealed. Over his shoulder he said, "You said you know about the Rotten Row ships, right?"

I nodded, all but running to keep as close to him as possible.

He said, "What I've heard—and I believe it—is the crimps hide the ones they kidnap on one of those empty ships. Who's going to be able to find them there? Can't search *all* of them, can you? Too many. Impossible. Kassel hides the ones he's sold on an empty ship till the last minute, before a departing boat sails off. That makes it safe for him. Safe for the captain on that ship. Understand now?"

"Is . . . is there anything to do against . . . against this Mr. Kassel?"

"You can be sure I'm *always* trying to think of that. Sometimes when we're playing he comes back and says, 'Play such and such for a particular customer.' You know what I do? I play it *badly*. Maybe he'll lose that customer and he'll go off. I know, it's not much, but it's something because Kassel holds all the power. Here you go," he said, turning around. "You're out of Happy Valley."

I couldn't move. "But . . . you're telling me my brother might be on one of those rotten ships and is . . . is about to be . . . stolen away."

"I'm not *telling* you anything. All I know is that's what Kassel does."

Altogether stunned, I said, "If Jacob is on some . . . Rotten Row ship . . . There are so many out there . . . How will I ever find him?"

Sam held out an open hand. "That's just what I'm saying. You probably can't. But if you do go looking, you'd better work fast, or you can say goodbye to Brother Jacob because you'll *never* find him. But I'll thank you, Miss Tory, not to say *one* word that it was me who told you all this. 'Cause if you do, I'll put my hand on twelve Bibles and swear you're lying. Understand? Good luck. And do me a favor: don't come back into the Mercury. And don't come back here to us either."

"Thank you," I mumbled as Sam turned around and took a step away.

"Sam," I called after him again. "Thank you."

He stopped.

I said, "Why . . . why did you tell me all this?"

He looked at me. "It's *not* for you. I *hate* Kassel. He's the devil in a tall hat. He stole my brother. Gone, just like I told you. No idea where he is. I'd do anything to work something against Kassel. Sometimes it feels like he has a whole army, and there is just me and my pa and we're a long way from home. Which," he added fiercely, "is why I keep playing that song. Wish I *were* home."

Before I could say any more, Sam disappeared into the jumble that was called Happy Valley. Which was not a valley and not happy.

·24·

JACOB *KIDNAPPED.* CRIMPED. STOLEN AWAY. TO say that I was shocked is too mild. I might as well use other words such as *dumbstruck, appalled,* and finally *helpless.* Never had I been so frightened. Except, the bigger truth was, I did not know what to do. Numb.

Some part of me did not even want to believe what Sam had suggested. It was too horrific. Or maybe he was just trying to get me to go away. Scare me off.

Next moment, I realized how much he *had* helped me. After all, he had been told *not* to speak to me by his father and by Mr. Kassel. But although Sam didn't owe me or Jacob anything, he *had* told me a great deal. At real risk. I was touched. Grateful.

There was something else: if I didn't want to believe it, the only way to prove Sam wrong was to find Jacob. Or have Jacob show up on his own. Otherwise, I had to believe Sam, didn't I? But if what Sam said was true? I must find Jacob ... *fast*. Or ... he'd disappear *forever*.

Wobbly, struggling for breath, trying desperately to think what I could do, I cannot say which hurt more: my head, stomach, or heart.

Somehow I made my way back into town. Once there, I went to Montgomery Street and stood on the edge of the cove. From that vantage point, I gazed out at the forsaken ships, which is to say Rotten Row.

The truth is, I had not spent much time thinking about the ships. Yes, they were there when our ship landed, and I had been curious about them, noticing that their numbers had much increased since we arrived. There were many hundreds now. But as far as I had been concerned, they were simply part of the madness that was San Francisco. Yes, odd. Truly strange. But not for a moment did I consider that they might have anything to do with *me*. Or Jacob.

But as I stood on the beach *that* moment and observed the empty ships, I saw the bulky, rotting hulks with altogether different eyes. It may seem fantastical, but crowded together as they were — some wedged so tightly I could have walked from one to another — they seemed alive, distressingly alive. Since the cove waters rippled some, the unoccupied ships shifted slightly, chafing and bumping one against another, making squeaking, grinding, and rasping sounds that reached the beach. It was almost as if the entire desolate fleet were some kind of wounded beast, masts, spars, and yards poking out in a million different ways, a bristled fiend-scathe or a gigantic multihorned and spiked but dying monster.

The idea that Jacob had been hidden away on *one* of those many ships — swallowed Jonah-like — was beyond horrifying. Because if it was true, how might I ever be able to find him?

Never in my life had I been so unnerved. I was absolutely sick. With my insides feeling like they were stuffed with stones, I stood there, more dead than alive. The more I stood there, trying to make up my mind (and control my feelings), the more I felt it was my fault that Jacob was gone. Knowing he had been unhappy, I should never, as Señor Rosales had gently hinted, have left him behind when I'd gone down the bay with Thad.

Let it be admitted: just the day before, I had pictured myself a grand *independent* adult. It had been wonderful to think I was free and liberated. Now I rued the moment. In truth, I'd grossly neglected my responsibilities. I had been arrogant. Do you wish to feel young? Be humiliated.

And what if Mother or Father returned and I could not tell them where Jacob was? The thought made me nauseous.

I *must* find Jacob.

Yet how?

I had no idea. Beyond all else, I felt terribly *alone*.

Next moment, I was overcome by an urgent need to speak to *someone*—as if to get away from my own frights. Yet understand: in San Francisco, other than in Happy Valley, there was no such thing as a neighborhood. It was not like Providence, where I knew everyone who lived on Sheldon Street as they knew me. Yes, the tents near us were occupied, but the young men who lived in them came and went like so many wispy clouds in the sky. As for women, there were so few, and if they were not at saloons, they ran boardinghouses or helped with a husband's business. I knew none. There was Señor Rosales, but he was overworked with his café. Who was I to turn to?

As you might have guessed, it was Thad.

I ran to the store where he worked and found him quick enough. He was clerking behind one of the counters, offering shovels and picks to a boisterous line of new arrivals.

Soon as he saw me, he called out, "Find him?"

Too agitated to talk, I merely shook my head.

He must have seen how troubled I was, because he said, "What happened?"

I wasn't going to repeat aloud what Sam had told me. I only said, "Come to my tent. Soon as you can."

"Will do."

I turned and fairly fled from the store, pushing my way through crowds of miners, who jeered and rebuked me for my belligerence. I did not care. I ran back uphill to our tent as fast as possible, forcing my way through the usual mobs. As I went, I kept repeating the same prayer in my head: *Be there. Be there. Oh, dear God, please let Jacob be there.*

I reached the tent and fairly well leaped inside.

Jacob was *not* there.

Whatever strength remained in me shrank to nothing. *Dissolved.* I flung myself onto Jacob's bed and burst into tears.

I beg you to understand; crying was something I *loathed*. But at that moment I could not help myself. I sobbed. My whole body trembled. My chest hurt. I could barely breathe. "What am I going to do?" I wailed aloud. "What am I going to do?"

I found Mother's shawl and wrapped it around me. How I missed her.

From across the way, I heard Señor Rosales call out. "Corderita, did you find him?" He must have seen me rush into the tent. Perhaps he'd heard my cries.

I sat up, worked to suppress my gulps of grief, and pawed at my wet face.

"Corderita," he called again, "what is it? What's the matter?"

Next moment, Señor Rosales did something he had never done before: he stuck his head into our tent.

"¿Que pasó? What did you learn about Jacob? What has happened?"

I looked up at him. My unhappy face must have revealed my ghastly feelings and frightened thoughts, because he came all the way in. More, he squatted down before me and put out a kind hand, which I clutched eagerly with both of mine, even as I wetted it with tears.

His gaze was full of sympathy. "Corderita, por favor, you must tell me. What's happened?"

Haltingly, now and again snuffling, struggling to keep from crumbling anew into sobs and tears, I told Señor Rosales all that Sam had told me and what I feared had happened to Jacob.

His face showed alarm and anger. "Santo Dios," he murmured, and made the sign of the cross over his chest more than once. "I have heard rumors of such terrible things," he said. "But . . . Jacob. Un niño. I warned your father. This place . . . Lobos. Sí. There are wolves here. Do you truly think that's what happened to him?"

Tears flowed down my cheeks. "I don't know," I wailed. "I just have to find him." It was hard for me to talk or breathe.

"Very well. On the square, the police chief—Señor Malachi Fallon—has his office in the old schoolhouse. There are police officers as well. Someone will help."

"Do you think so?"

"Corderita, Señor Fallon is la policía. He must find Jacob. It's his obligation. Come, I'll go with you."

"Will you?" I said, deeply grateful for his help.

"Corderita, I have told you many times: I think of you as my daughter. Jacob, my son. My daughter isn't here because, as I told your esteemed padre, this city is not safe for young people. Forgive me. His leaving you was a mistake. This proves me right. But since you are my local daughter, well, then, I will help."

I jumped up and hugged him. He hugged me back.

"Vamos," he said. "Now we must find Señor Fallon. As that boy Sam told you, if all of this is true, we must act rápidamente."

"Señor," I said, "one thing. You cannot say anything about Sam."

"Why?

"He's worried that he will be blamed."

"Fine. Whatever you say. Now we must hurry."

·25·

WE SQUISHED THROUGH THE MUD TO PORTS-mouth Square, going right to the old schoolhouse, a small, single-story wooden building. When we reached it, I stood next to Señor Rosales at the front door, trying to catch my breath and unclutter my thoughts.

"What do you wish to do?" he asked me. "I can talk to whoever is here. But perhaps it's better that you do. Jacob is your hermano."

It may seem stupid to say, or even simple, but I was learning that being frightened while trying to decide the right thing to do is difficult. I struggled hard to control my distress. "I'll talk," I said, and forced myself to stand straight and wipe the tears from my face. "I'm ready," I said, though I didn't think I was.

"Bueno. Think for a moment what you will say."

I took a deep breath. Then nodded.

Señor Rosales pushed the door open.

It was a large room, divided in half, front and back, with a door to the back part. Next to the door was a bench with a man sitting on it. He was bent over reading the *Alta California,* the newspaper for which Thad's father worked.

When we came in, this man looked up. His weather-beaten face bore a large and crooked nose, as if it had been broken some while ago. The skin about his small eyes was puffy, his mouth set in a frown, his chin neither smooth nor bearded, while his thick hair was much disheveled. A large pistol was stuck in his belt.

In short: there was something altogether disagreeable about him.

Señor Rosales spoke first. "Señor, con respecto, where is the police chief?"

The man looked at me and then at Señor Rosales. He appeared to be one of those people who take time to speak, not because he is thinking but to show you he's in charge. When he did respond, he nodded toward the door, saying, "Don't know if he's there."

"Why?" I said.

"He don't answer to me." With that, the man shook out the paper as if it contained crumbs that needed disposing of. Then he made a demonstration of resuming his reading.

Ignoring him, I went forward and knocked on the door. No one answered. I looked at Señor Rosales. He pursed his lips. I looked at the man with the newspaper. Though he kept his eyes fixed on the paper, I was sure he was not reading but waiting to see what I did.

Agitated, desperate to do *something*, I twisted the big doorknob and pushed the door open.

There was a big oaken desk in the middle of this smaller room, plus a few large chairs. On the wall hung a picture of James Polk, the former president of the United States, the one whose words had brought my father and thousands of others to California.

A man behind the desk was leaning forward, his head resting in his arms. Judging by his heavy, steady breathing, he was asleep.

I shoved the door farther in, went forward, and stood before the desk. "Sir," I said, trying to keep my voice steady.

The man didn't move. I looked at Señor Rosales. He shrugged.

"Captain Fallon," I called, louder. When he didn't stir, I leaned over the desk. "Captain Fallon, sir. Hello."

Very slowly, the man sat up, revealing a square, fleshy face with bags under small, sleepy eyes. His mouth was thin-lipped, and he had a high, receding hairline topped with thin, curly hair. He looked first at Señor Rosales and then at me as if struggling to grasp that we were even there.

"Sir," I said, "I need help."

"Well, now," he muttered, rubbing his face, "and what might be the kind of help you're asking for?"

"Please, sir," I said again. "Are you Captain Fallon? The police chief?"

"It's what I'm called."

"Please, I really need help."

"Do you?" He took a deep breath, and his baleful eyes considered me with as much sympathy as if I were a stray dog.

I said, "I think my brother has been kidnapped."

Captain Fallon barely reacted. He simply clasped his large hands before him and continued to sit there as if not interested, or perhaps not understanding. "And who is your brother?"

"Jacob Blaisdell."

"Young, old?

"Ten."

"Ah," he said, and actually yawned. "Just a lad. Who are you and what's your age?"

"I'm Victoria Blaisdell. I'm fourteen."

"A girl."

The way he said it was dismissive. "This man"—he nodded to Señor Rosales—"who is he?"

"A friend. He's helping me. My father is at the diggings."

"Where's your ma?"

"She'll be here any day now. From back east."

"You're alone, then?"

"Yes, sir."

Captain Fallon studied his hands, then sighed as if bored. "Have you," he said, without looking up, "any idea how many people, every day, go missing from this city?"

"No, sir," I said.

"And ninety-nine out of a hundred have only taken themselves off to the gold fields."

"Jacob wouldn't do that."

The man's sleepy eyes lifted and studied me for a while. "All right, then," he said, as if obliged, "tell me about your brother."

As I repeated what Sam had told me, Mr. Fallon's face screwed up into a scowl.

"Who told you all that?"

"A boy."

"What boy?"

"A Negro boy who plays bugle at the Mercury," I blurted out. "He lives in Happy Valley."

"Colored boy, you say? At the Mercury? What makes you so sure he's telling the truth?"

"Because I trust him and my brother is gone."

Next moment, I realized what I'd done: exactly what Sam had asked me *not* to do, reveal him as the source of my information.

Captain Fallon frowned. "How long has your brother been missing?"

"A day."

"One day . . ." He passed a hand over his face as if wiping away sleep or my remarks. "Look here. Listen to me. This brother of yours, he most likely went off to have a bit of fun. It's what boys do. You needn't worry none. If I were you, I'd go about your business. He'll be coming back."

"But, sir . . ."

"You said your father is at the diggings. Have you considered that your brother went looking for him?"

"I don't think—"

"What's your name again?"

"Victoria Blaisdell."

He considered me with cloudy eyes. "Well, now, I'll tell you what, Miss Victoria: if your brother don't come back in a few days, you be sure to let me know."

"But—"

"For now, no more."

With that, Captain Fallon lowered his head back into his arms. In seconds, I heard his heavy, steady breathing. He was not just telling us to go; he had gone back to sleep. Or he was pretending to. Furious, I walked out of the office.

As we came out, the man on the bench glanced up at me from his newspaper. The door to Chief Fallon's office having remained open, I wondered if this man had overheard my conversation. Not that he said anything to me, or I to him. He returned to his newspaper as if what he was reading was more interesting than me.

The moment Señor Rosales and I were out of the building, I cried, "Jacob did *not* go off for fun. And he didn't go to the diggings. Not without telling me."

"I don't think so either," Señor Rosales replied. As we started back toward the tent, he kept one hand on my shoulder, as if to steady me. We had to work our way through crowds.

After a while I said, "I have to search those ships."

He halted. "What ships?"

"Rotten Row."

"The abandoned ones?"

"Yes."

He looked downhill, toward the cove. "Corderita, there are so many. Cientos. Hundreds. That isn't smart. I don't call you corderita—little lamb—for nothing. Lobos. Wolves. Don't forget the lobos."

"But . . . what else am I to do?" I cried, struggling yet again to keep back tears. Ashamed, I turned away. For a moment

I thought I saw that man—the one in the police office. Was he following us? I trusted nothing. At that moment, Señor Rosales touched my shoulder. I swung around to face him.

"Maybe Jacob will come back on his own. After all, *you* broke your oar when you went down the bay, but you still managed to return."

"Jacob doesn't *do* things like that. He's . . . he's timid. And I told that man about Sam!" I cried. "I promised I wouldn't."

"I am not sure, corderita, the police chief listened to anything you said."

I looked back to see if that man was behind us. If it had been him, he was no longer there. I decided I was just inventing more problems. Increasingly unnerved, I started up walking again. I did not speak. It was raining.

Señor Rosales said, "Muy bien. Search. But you can't search those empty ships alone. It will be not safe. And the rain . . ."

"I have to."

"I'm the adulto here. I'll go with you."

"You can't leave your café. You don't have doors."

"Have faith, corderita. People will not steal. Besides, Jacob . . . and you are más importantes."

"Gracias," I returned, feeling it deeply. But I had no patience to listen. What I wanted to do was immediately go to those empty ships. Yes, there were hundreds, but I was convinced Jacob was in one of them.

We walked the rest of the way back in silence. The rain stopped and started again. Not that I cared. *You must find Jacob* was the thought that repeated itself over and over again in my head. *You must.*

·26·

WHEN WE APPROACHED OUR TENT, I SAW THAD sitting on the ground, waiting. As soon as he saw us, he scrambled to his feet. "I'm here," he called.

As we drew near, Señor Rosales realized he had customers waiting at his café. "Un momento. I'll be back," he said, and went off to serve them.

"Come out of the rain," I said to Thad, and went into the tent. I sat down on our box table. Thad sat on Jacob's bed. Facing him, holding my arms tightly about my chest, I poured out everything I knew, what Sam had said, how kind Señor Rosales was, but that the police offered nothing, at least not for a few days. "But by then," I added, "it might be too late." Once again, my tears were streaming.

Thad listened openmouthed. When I'd finished talking, he said, "You really think Jacob got crimped?"

"I do!" I cried. "I don't know what else to believe. Jacob wouldn't just go away. I know that. Someone stole him. And if Sam is right, I have to find him *fast*."

"Nice that kid Sam told you."

"It was. Except he asked me not to say anything about him. And I did."

"Who to?"

"Señor Rosales. The police chief. You. Being upset makes me stupid. I *hate* being stupid," I fairly shouted. "I should never have left Jacob alone." I smeared the tears from my face.

Thad shifted about with discomfort. Then he said, "All right, then, what are we going to do about it?"

I heard that "we" and was ever grateful.

I said, "I have to go to the cove and search Rotten Row."

"There are hundreds of ships."

"Thad," I cried, "I have to find him!" I think I was yelling at myself.

Thad looked at me, got up, and said, "OK. Let's go."

I was not going to argue. "Un momento," I said, and hurried out of the tent and to the café. Señor Rosales was working, cooking and serving meals to a line of men.

"Lo siento," he called to me.

"Thad said he'd go right now with me to the ships."

"Excelente. I'll join you when I can."

By the time Thad and I headed downhill, it was late afternoon. He, as usual, said little, and I was spent of words. If anything, his impatient, long legs carried him faster. I was fine with hurrying, working hard to just breathe.

The rain had stopped, but the wind was astir, making the air cold. Would San Francisco ever be warm? As we rushed along, I kept my eyes on the cove ships and had to admit what everyone was cautioning: there *were* so many. And a fair number were huge. It truly was overwhelming. But it was also maddening to think that by gazing upon the rotten fleet, I was, in all probability, looking at where Jacob was being hidden, yet I couldn't know which ship held him.

How, then, to begin? How to pick the first ship to search? I was reminded of something I once read: "If you look at everything, you see nothing."

Then I told myself, *I'm doing something,* and struggled to soothe myself by thinking, *It's better doing than dithering.* I was desperate to begin, my nerves as tight as fiddle strings, though there was no music coming from me.

When we reached the cove, Thad went right to the rowboat we had used to go down the bay. Happily, both oars were there. But I also saw that the tide was rising, which would hinder the rowing. We shoved the small boat into the water. The sound of it grating over the sand made me shiver.

I scrambled onto the rowboat's center seat and snatched up the oars.

"Where are we starting?" Thad asked as he gave us another shove farther out and climbed into the stern seat.

I looked over my shoulder at the mass of desolate ships and realized I wished that someone might just say, "Go to *that* brig, the one with the tattered flying jib hanging from its bowsprit." Or "It's that three-masted frigate with a broken angel figurehead."

Needless to say, no one said anything of the kind. Instead, I sat motionless, overwhelmed by what I was wanting— needing—to do, while knowing that time was crucial and flowing fast, like the tide.

Thad came to my rescue. "Let's try that small one." He pointed. "See her? On the edge."

I saw the boat he meant: a small vessel, not nearly as big as the others in the fleet. She had but one mainmast, plus what they call a mizzen at the stern.

Relieved to have a direction with which to begin the search, I began to row, though I was too fraught to labor well. Each time the oars hit the water, they splashed noisily, making us jerk forward so that my braid kept whipping around, bothering my face. I had to struggle to keep my hands under control. In fact, they were trembling. My eyes hurt with suppressed tears.

Thad, impatient, held out his hands, telling me he was willing to row. Annoyed, I snapped, "I can do it. Just tell me where to go. What kind of boat is it?" I asked, trying to ease the tension.

"It's what they call a ketch," he said as we moved along with greater ease. "Bet she came down from Oregon. The sails are only halfway lowered. Her crew—two, three? Ayuh. They couldn't get off her fast enough."

I looked around and saw the boat he meant. There was a sign tacked to her bow that read OFF FOR RICHES. HELP YOURSELF.

We drew close. I used one oar to swing our boat about until the stern bumped up against the ketch's hull. Thad stood, reached up, found a grip hold, and pulled us closer.

"Jacob," I shouted. "Jacob, it's me, Tory. Jacob!"

There was no answer.

Thad grabbed a loose line and pulled. It proved long enough to tie to our rowboat so as to keep her from floating off.

"I'll board her," he said, and he reached for the bulwark rail and began to haul himself up.

"Wait! I'm coming too." I shipped the oars.

As soon as Thad was on the deck, he turned around and held out his hand. Unsteady in the bobbing rowboat, I grabbed it, and he pulled. Although awkward, the next moment, I was standing next to him on the deck.

The ketch was small and open, with most of her deck before the main mast. Many lines lay about, some looking like birds' nests, others coiled with care. A good number of tools, like a belaying pin and a mallet, were strewn about. An anchor line hung from her bow and kept her in place. I wondered why they'd bothered. She felt desolate and empty.

The boat was odd to see. Though we knew that she had no crew and had been left behind, she had her full rig of sails. They hung limply from her two masts. The lower edge of the mizzen sail dipped into the water and was stained with green scum.

There was a hatchway to some space below deck.

"She's all here," said Thad. "Sign says we could take her and sail around the world. We should do it."

"That's not why we're here," I said, frustrated by his bantering. I went to the hatchway and leaned over it. "Jacob!" I called.

There was no answer.

Dim though it was, I could see deep enough below to be sure no one was there.

I pulled myself up. "Not here," I announced.

Thad said, "Let's try another ship."

·27·

W E SCAMPERED OFF THE KETCH AND BACK INTO the rowboat. I looked about, trying to decide where, among all those ships, to go next. Once again, the sheer number of them and their size fed my anguish, while the increasing dusk only added to my misery. It would be dark soon.

"I'm betting on that one," said Thad, pointing to the nearest ship. She was a two-masted brig. Tattered gray sails sagged from her foremast, suggesting nothing so much as exhaustion.

I began to row. Once close, I backed against the brig, stern first. The ship made our rowboat feel tiny.

"Can we get on?" I asked, looking up. The top rail was quite some ways above us.

"I'm able," said Thad. "She's not that high. Just have to gaffle these ratlines." He grabbed the dangling web of ropes—they were like loose ladders—and began to climb. In moments, he disappeared over the topgallant rail, gone briefly before his head popped up. "Not hard," he called.

I tied our rowboat to the brig, and then followed him up to the deck. It worked my muscles, but I succeeded.

Like the ketch, the brig's main deck was in complete disorder. She was not just derelict but looked as if she had just been ransacked. For a moment, my spirits lifted. If other people had been on her recently, maybe they had brought Jacob here and left him.

It was easy enough to see he was not on deck. We searched the deck structures too, a few small cabins which for the most part had been ripped open, some of the wood removed, I supposed, for building in town. It didn't matter what these cabins had been used for; Jacob was not in them.

We came to the companionway steps that led to the ship's lower decks. I lay on my stomach and stared into the blackness below. Cupping my mouth, I shouted, "Jacob! Jacob! Are you there? It's me, Tory."

No answer.

I went down, every step bringing me deeper into darkness. "Jacob!"

I descended farther only to hold back. It wasn't just murky; the smell was foul.

"Don't get lost there," Thad called.

I went on. The darkness grew deeper, the stink worse. I began to hear faint rustlings, plus some high-pitched squeaks. Something ran over my foot. "Oh," I cried, and leaped up a step, my body shuddering.

"What?" Thad called.

"Rats, I think."

"Maybe you don't want to go anymore."

"Jacob!" I yelled as loud as I could. "Are you here?"

Other than a faint echo, there was no response. I retreated to the main deck and took a deep breath.

Twilight had come. The city hills were glittery with points of candle, lantern, and cooking fires—as if stars had fallen and become stuck in its mud.

Thad said, "Should have brought a lantern."

I stood in place, full of ache, breathing hard with distress. I didn't know what to do.

"We'll come back tomorrow," said Thad.

Not answering, I went to the rail and stared out over Rotten Row. The multitude of ships—massive, mute, and dark—seemed positively evil to me.

I had no voice to speak. I wanted to cry. I didn't.

Thad came up to my side, "He's here somewhere. We'll find him."

"Hope," I managed to say, then added, "Thank you for helping."

"Ayuh," he said. "Best friends." Then he said, "Better get back to the beach."

"Thad," I said, "my father is due from the diggings."

"When?"

"In a few days."

"Ayuh," he said again. I wondered how many meanings the one word — or sound — had.

"What am I going to say to him? Just, 'Jacob's gone. It's my fault. Sorry.'?"

Thad shook his head. "According to Sam, you didn't lose him. Someone took him."

"It's horrible."

"What difference does it make? He's gone."

Fumbling, working hard not to slip and fall midst all the deck clutter, we got off the ship and into the rowboat. This time Thad took the oars. I sat in the stern, hugging myself against the chill, tense with frustration.

Without talking, Thad kept looking over his shoulder as he rowed. As we drew in, I could see someone on the shore, as if waiting for us.

It was Sam. He was standing there, bugle under his arm.

"I was going over to the Mercury," he called as we drew in, "when I saw people out in Rotten Row. I was wondering if it was you. This your brother?" He meant Thad.

I shook my head. "My friend Thaddeus." I turned to Thad.

"This is Samuel. Sam. He's the one who told me about crimping."

Thad made a friendly nod but, in his way, didn't say anything.

"*Were* you searching?" Sam asked me.

"A couple of the boats. But it got too dark."

"You need light."

As Thad and I pulled the rowboat up onto the beach, Sam stood there as if not sure what to do. For a moment, Thad hung back, then he went up to Sam, hand out. "Thanks for telling Tory about crimping," he said, then added, "I'm Thad."

Sam shifted his bugle under his arm, shook Thad's hand, and nodded. "It's not good."

Thad said, "Really think Jacob got kidnapped?"

Sam looked at me. "You were in my tent. You notice how many beds there were?"

"Three."

"One belongs to that brother I told you about."

Thad said, "What happened to him?"

"One night he vanished. From the Mercury. Just like her brother."

"Whoa," said Thad.

"Don't know for certain, but we're pretty sure. Disappeared in September. Crimped. Not a trace."

I stared at him. "No idea where?"

Sam shook his head.

Thad said, "Did you tell the police?"

"They're not about to help colored folk."

"That's awful," I said, even as I recognized the weakness of my words.

Sam said, "That's why I told you about Kassel. Don't want it to happen to your bother. Or anyone."

"Jacob's a kid," said Thad. He turned to me. "How old?"

"Ten."

"Can't see what use he'd be."

"Ship boy," said Sam. "Some people, let me tell you, they like to be waited on. Can make a man feel important."

I heard his deep anger. Not knowing what to say, I turned my back on the boys and stared out at the Rotten Row ships. Faint as they were, I couldn't take my eyes from them. As I thought, *Jacob is there, somewhere*, I hated them.

"You going to search some more?" asked Sam.

Thad said, "Too dark."

Sam said, "I might be able to get a lantern at the Mercury. Take a few minutes."

I turned about. "Thank you," I said, grateful.

"But going on those ships at night," said Sam, "it'll be dangerous." Then he lifted his bugle. "I've got to work."

"I'll walk with you," Thad said to Sam.

"One thing," said Sam. "I don't want Kassel seeing me with

you at the Mercury." He turned to Thad. "She"—he meant me—"explain who that is?"

Thad nodded.

I felt a stab of guilt.

"Let's go, then," said Sam.

"Sam," I called out, "I made a bad mistake."

"What?"

"I went to the police—Chief Fallon. I thought he might help me find Jacob. I told him he might have been crimped. When he asked me how I knew that, I was so upset that I let it slip that it was you who told me."

The light might have been dim, but I could see Sam's face fill with anger. "You *told* him about me?"

I nodded.

Sam spun away.

Mortified, I called, "I'm sorry. It was wrong of me. I . . . I hope nothing bad comes of it."

"Me too," I heard Sam say. He was still not looking at me. To Thad he said, "Come on. Let's go." His voice had changed. It wasn't friendly. I felt awful.

The two of them started to walk away. I wanted them to be friends. I could hear Thad say, "That's ghastly 'bout your brother. I'm from Maine. Bath. Where you from?"

I got back into the rowboat and sat on the center seat, staring bleakly out over the cove. I was angry at myself for betraying Sam and wondered if he would talk to me again. What if my talking to the police made more trouble for him? I thought of Jacob as well. Was he in a cabin on one of those ships? In the hold . . . ? Was he tied up? Did he have anything to eat? Did he know I was looking for him?

There I was, a fourteen-year-old, and for the *first* time in my life I was not just upset but mortified, deeply disappointed, not liking myself. I liked to think of myself as older, wiser. I was older, maybe, but obviously not wiser. Is distress the best teacher? Or pain? I had both. I had the thought: *Does knowing you aren't wise make you wise?*

As I sat there, trying to sort my emotions, I heard footsteps crunch on the beach behind me. Startled, I spun around.

·28·

IT WAS SEÑOR ROSALES, CANDLE IN HAND.
"¡Corderita! Is that you? Did you find Jacob?"

Though glad to see him, I shook my head.

He came up to me. The candle lit his face enough for me
to see his concern. "What did you do?"

I said, "We searched two ships. But it got dark, so Thad
went to get a lantern."

"I have spoken to some friends. I hate to tell you, but
they believe that Señor Fallon — the man we saw, the chief of
la policía — he knows all about this business — this crimping."

"The police chief?" I cried.

"It's what I was told. That he, or his officers, take some of
the money paid for those who've been stolen. Sobornos. Bribes.

Same thing. I can't say for sure. Do you wish me to walk you back to the tent?"

"Thad is returning. We're going to search some more."

"¿En la noche?"

"He's getting a lantern. I have to keep looking."

"Please, corderita, con cuidado—be careful."

"We will."

He hesitated, and then said, "Let me see you in the morning. Please, con cuidado. Otherwise I will worry. Buenas noches. I pray you find him." He made a cross over his chest.

"Buenas noches, señor."

I watched him as he moved away into the dark.

As I continued to sit in the rowboat, I thought about what he had told me, that the police might be involved in the kidnapping. Is there anything more appalling than believing that the people you think can help—should help—are your enemies? And what can one do when all you have is questions and no answers? And what if your brother's life depends on getting at least one right answer? And what if my parents show up and the first thing they say is "Where's your brother?"

I sat there feeling small and cold, not wanting to think because only bad thoughts came. Too many what-ifs.

"Tory!"

With a start, I turned. Along the shore, I saw a bobbing

glow coming in my direction. "Got light." It was Thad. He lifted up a lantern.

I climbed out of the rowboat. Thad set his lantern into it. "Let's go," he said.

"Do you think we should try now, in the dark?"

"I thought we had to."

"We do," I said.

The two of us shoved the boat into the cold water, getting our feet wet.

I took up the oars and began to row.

"How's Sam?" I asked.

"Finest kid," said Thad, *finest* being his highest compliment.

"Is he angry at me?"

"Wasn't happy. Did say if we didn't find Jacob tonight, he might help tomorrow during the day. Works at night."

Thad held up the lit lantern and stared out into the cove. "He had to come out of the Mercury to give me the lantern." He looked over his shoulder to me. "Tory, he's really worried about that Mr. Kassel. You shouldn't have said anything to the police."

I stopped rowing.

Thad said, "He's sure that Kassel stole his brother. Sold him into slavery."

"That's horrible," I said. "I wish I could help."

"Wishing is what little kids do."

His words stung. I had said something like that to my father. Knowing Thad was right made the pain worse.

After a moment, I said, "Señor Rosales came down here. He thinks the police know about the crimping. That they're part of it, make money from it."

"He know for sure?"

"Not exactly," I said.

Thad looked at me. I could see he was troubled.

"Thad," I said, "I have to know. Am I doing everything wrong?"

"You're trying to do what's right. I'll give you that. Lot of folks don't even try. Hey, if you don't put something down on the table you won't ever win."

Feeling miserable, wrathy at myself, I took a deep breath and began to row. The plash of oars was steady. I kept thinking about Sam's brother. And Jacob. I was tired of *saying*. I, who loved words, felt I'd used too many. Just wanting to *do,* I kept rowing.

Our lantern light didn't reveal much. The cove water was black, made a little choppy by a rising wind, which whispered low and breathy, reminding me of a sick person. Overhead, dark, skimming clouds hid the stars and an almost-full moon. Some light came out of the city, scattering sparks here and there upon the water's surface. Spits of cold rain sometimes fell and made me shiver. I wished I had my mother's shawl.

After a while I said, "Where are we going?"

"Another ship."

I sighed. "Just tell me where."

Thad held up his lantern.

We were out into the cove, which was crowded with dead ships, their masts and spars a leafless forest, vanishing into the high darkness.

"That one," said Thad, pointing.

"Why?"

He shrugged. "Closest."

I stared into the darkness and saw the ship's hulking shape. In moments, my oar strokes brought us up against its hull with a bump.

This ship was much bigger than the two we had already searched, soaring over our heads like a mountain cliff. When I looked up, I could barely see her masts—two, maybe three— which slid into the murky gloom. The wet wind whispered through her rigging.

I edged around the ship, looking for a ladder or a line such as we had used before. At first we found nothing, but finally Thad's lantern revealed some drooping ropes, long enough so that they trailed into the water. He gave yanks to a few of them. One fell into the water and lay there like a coiled snake, only to sink.

It took a while, but he found a line that held fast when

he pulled hard. He fastened its loose and slippery end to our rowboat so it would not float away.

I glanced toward the shore but could no longer see it. It was as if we were nowhere. "How are we going to do this?" I asked, peering up.

Thad said, "You hold the lantern. I'll climb the line. Think you can follow?"

"Thad, I'm going first." It came out angrily, but it was annoyance at myself for having nothing but bad thoughts.

Thad said nothing, for which I was thankful. I said, "When I get on deck I'll find another line to bring up the lantern. We're going to need light. Then you come." I was talking as if I knew what I was doing. I didn't really feel that way. I just wanted to move.

"I suppose," Thad replied. I could hear his doubt and it bothered me.

Not wishing to think too much, I reached as high on the line as I could and grabbed it with two hands, grateful that it wasn't wet and slimy.

I began by giving the line a hard tug to make sure it would not come free. It held. Then, sucking in a deep breath and using all the strength I could muster, I hoisted my whole body, until my legs lifted off our rowboat. Next I swung my legs *in,* so that my booted feet were flat on the side planking of the ship.

With my arms holding my full weight, I moved my hands

one over the other, hauling higher each time. Thus I tugged myself upward, hand over hand, bit by bit, so that I actually walked up the side of the ship. The line was rough, my hands hurt, I was breathing fast, but I didn't slip. I dared not. It helped that the ship's hull was cankered — full of edges — which allowed my booted feet to gain purchase. All the strength from the hard labor I had done the past few months helped.

I tried not to think what I was doing, only that I was going up. The higher I went, the darker it became. It was as if I were climbing into the night. The farther I climbed, the greater the ache in my arms, making me think my body would pull out of my shoulders.

At one point my hauling was so agonizing, I considered finding relief by letting go. But I'd reached such a height that I was equally fearful of doing anything but continuing. I was afraid to look up. Or down.

Accepting that I had little choice save climbing, I pulled hand over hand, moving up inch by inch. The ship had seemed large when I first saw it. Now it felt gigantic.

I continued to yank and walk, yank and walk, step by step, until I came within reach of the topgallant rail. By then I was hiddy-giddy, my breath popping in puffs, my arms and sides in jangling pain. The only light, blurry in my tear-filled eyes, came from Thad's lantern far below.

The last moment was hardest. And agonizing. I pulled my right hand away from the line, which meant I was holding my entire weight with my left hand. Then I grabbed the topgallant rail of the ship with my free, right hand, let go of the line, and as fast as anything I did in all my life, shifted my left hand onto the railing. Now, at least, I was hanging with *two* hands.

Heaving, pulling, and lugging desperately, I yanked myself up and over the rail, then tumbled down onto the other side of the bulwark, where I landed on the deck with a hard *thud*.

For what seemed a long time, I just lay there, my breath coming in rapid, shredded huffs. There was nothing but hurt inside and outside my body. I felt nauseous. My arms burned. My fingers numb and raw. I licked a finger. I think I tasted blood. Happily, it was so dark I couldn't see.

"You all right?" I heard Thad shout. His voice came as if from a great distance.

I pulled myself up until I was standing, albeit shakily, and looked down over the rail. Thad was standing in the boat, looking up from what seemed to be a deep and narrow well of pale-yellow light.

"Tory? You all right?"

It wasn't true, but I shouted, "Fine."

"Get something to bring up the lantern."

I looked about. It was hard to see much of anything. Then

I saw, dimly, a tangled coil of line at my feet. I grabbed it and threw it over. I watched as Thad took hold of the end and tied it to the handle loop of the lantern.

"Pull her," he called, which I did, halfway up the hull.

"I'll keep it there so you can climb," I shouted, and tied the line off. "Can you walk up the way I did? Use the line I used. It should hold."

"I will," he yelled, and began to walk up the side of the ship.

At one point, he skidded—I think he was trying to move too fast, and his feet went off the hull. For a few moments, he dangled in the air, swinging like a clock's pendulum.

My heart squeezed.

Somehow he managed to hitch himself around, threw his feet forward, secured a firm tread and a tighter grip on the line, then once again, he continued up.

It was as hard for him as it was for me. The big difference being that, at the last moment, when he was in reach, I hung over the topgallant rail, grabbed his wrists, and helped bring him aboard.

In moments, we were standing side by side on the ship's main deck. Thad's breath came in short gulps.

I was thinking, *This is too hard,* but I knew there were harder things to come.

·29·

T HAD SAID, "I SLIPPED. SCARY."

"You got here," I replied, not wanting to talk about it. Instead I hauled up the lantern.

The lantern's light enabled us to survey the ship's deck. It was desolate and disorderly, with all manner of things strewn about: lines, wood, boxes, and broken barrels. Overhead, squinny and scranny masts and spars spiked up and away. The only sounds I heard were the ship's timbers, grating and groaning, the way I imagined a person might sound when in slow and dying agony.

I thought, *All these ships have been left to rot. But it's not the ships that are rotten. What's rotten is leaving them for gold.*

"Come on," I said, whispering, though why I whispered I wasn't sure, save that it was an under-breathy kind of place.

Staying close to each other, lantern held before us, we walked about the upper deck with care.

We went from bow to stern and back again, searching as much as we could, trying to make sure we did not trip on litter and refuse. Our footsteps made squeaky creaks upon the deck planks.

At one point, I stopped and cried out, "Jacob! Jacob!"

No reply.

We found an open hatchway, the steps leading steeply down. I leaned over it, shining the lantern into the darkness.

"Jacob. Are you there? It's me. Tory. Jacob!" It made my throat hurt to scream so. The only reply was an empty echo of my own voice.

I tried to decide if I should go below.

Thad, as if reading my mind, said, "We should check down there."

I leaned over the hatchway again. "Jacob!" I yelled, as loud as I could.

No answer.

I told myself there had to be many rooms, berths, and cabins on the lower deck. If Jacob was trapped, or confined there, the only way to find him was to go down.

A rope banister was slung along one side of the steps. Holding the lantern in one hand, the rope with the other, I took perhaps fifteen steps down until I was a few feet above the lower deck. Thad came down right behind me.

The lantern light allowed me to look into a vast, empty cavern, the cross timbers looking like the ribs of some enormous, hollow beast. Against the port and starboard side were multiple sleeping berths. Everything empty. It made me think of a cemetery with nothing but open, unfilled graves.

The lower deck was another confusion of boxes and barrels. And rats. I saw their eyes—like hot embers—reflecting the glow of my lantern. Impossible to count their numbers. My light or shouting must have disturbed them because the deck floor fairly quivered with these dirty, revolting beasts, with their constant high-pitched squeaks. The thought that Jacob might be down among them made me queasy.

"Jacob!" I yelled again.

The rats scurried, the patter of their tiny feet enough to raise goose bumps on my arms.

I waited for a reply, any reply. None came. Just rats.

"He's not here," I said, and backed up. Thad went before me.

Without saying anything, we returned to the rail where we had come aboard. Trying not to sound defeated and dirty, which is how I felt, I said, "We need to try another ship."

Thad said. "I'll go down first. Catch you if you fall."

Irritated, I said, "I'm not going to fall."

I held the lantern over the topgallant rail. Thad grasped our climbing line and hoisted himself onto the rail. For a moment, he sat there then flipped over onto his belly with his feet hanging over the side. Using two hands, he slid down until his head disappeared. I watched him as he went, moving a lot faster than when he had come up.

He reached our rowboat. "I'm here!" he yelled.

Using another line, I lowered the lantern into his hands. He held it up so I could see where I needed to go.

"I'm coming," I called, and grabbed the same line he had used. First I hoisted myself to the topgallant rail, and then let my feet dangle over nothing. Gripping the line as tightly in my two hands as I could, I spun about and began to descend.

When I had come up, hard as it was, I hadn't considered how much harder it would be going the other way. Now, my weight pulled at me as if I had gained a hundred pounds. My body wanted to drop. My brain told me I must not. I might land in the water, and I could not swim.

I tried to descend hand over hand, but the palms of my hands burned. And then, after I had gone down no more than a third of the way, Thad's lantern light went dark.

Clinging to the line, I hung there, unable to see anything. "Thad!" I screamed.

"Right here."

"What happened?"

"Oil must have been used up. You all right?"

"No! Keep talking. I've got to keep coming."

I started going down again, moving slower than before, which was also more painful. I had no idea how far I was above the water and Thad.

I paused. I swayed.

"Are you there?" I yelled. "Talk."

Next moment, Thad began to sing:

> *"You're crowded in with dirty men*
> *As fattening hogs are in a pen,*
> *And what will more a man provoke*
> *Is musty plug tobacco smoke.*
> *The ladies are compelled to sit*
> *With dresses in tobacco spit.*
> *The gentlemen don't seem to care*
> *But talk of politics as they swear.*

"You're close," he shouted. Next moment, I felt his hands on my boots. My relief was so great that my grip on the line gave way, and I tumbled, falling on top of Thad, so we both went floundering in the bottom of our rowboat. It rocked wildly, shipping some water.

We lay there, too skeery to move, until the boat became

steady. I pushed myself up. All I could think to say was "Why were you singing that song?"

"So you'd know where I was."

"Where'd you ever learn it?"

"Don't know. Think it's funny."

"It's not," I said, except my respite from fright was so great that I started to laugh. Then he laughed too. Our sense of safety made us giddy.

We got onto the boat seats. I rubbed my arms. "That was almost impossible."

"Right gory," he agreed. "Ready to try another boat?"

I did want to. But I said, "Not without a lantern. We need to get extra oil and a flint. Let's get to shore."

Though my hands felt raw, once our rowboat was set free, I pulled up the oars and headed us back to the cove beach. Gradually, light from the city allowed us to make our way. I was glad to be rowing; the steady strokes freed up my muscles.

Within minutes we were on shore and had the boat hauled up. We stood there, staring out at the ghostly fleet. Glad to be on land, I realized I was completely worn out. My legs felt weak.

"I can't do any more," I said, disappointed in myself. "In the morning, early, we can look some more."

"Sure," Thad said. "Do you think Jacob could be somewhere other than the ships?"

"Sam seems to know what he's talking about," I said. Then I added, "Thank you for your help," full of gratitude but not knowing how to say or show it beyond simple words.

"Ayuh," said Thad. He lifted the lantern. "Should get this back to Sam. He's probably still at the Mercury."

I was too tired to talk as we started walking, going along Montgomery Street until we reached the Central Wharf. Once there, we headed out, finding it crowded with shouting and carousing miners. Many were slovenly with drink, San Francisco at its worst. We had to push and squeeze our way through the maelstrom of men.

As we approached the entrance to the Mercury, there were two men having a fistfight. A crowd had gathered round them and while the men were bloodying each other, the onlookers were clearly enjoying it, encouraging the men to fight harder. It is difficult to say what this violence did more: disgust or frighten me.

Thad and I moved away, but I could not take my eyes from the fight or the men who had gathered round. It was ugly. *Why are you watching?* I asked myself even as I continued doing so.

"We going in?" Thad asked me after a moment.

I shook my head. "I shouldn't be here. Sam was warned about talking to me."

"Warned about *talking*?"

I nodded. "Because I'm white."

Thad shook his head.

"That's what he said."

"Who warned him?"

"That Mr. Kassel."

"The crimp?"

I nodded.

Thad, glowering, stood looking at the Mercury as if he could see the man.

"I may have already done harm talking with the police," I reminded him. "Sam doesn't need me to make things harder."

Thad lifted the lantern. "What about this?"

"You bring it. Kassel doesn't know you."

Thad considered me for a moment and then said, "Be back fast as I can." He disappeared into the Mercury while I stood on the far side of the wharf.

I waited, my eyes going from the ongoing fight to the entrance to the Mercury, wanting Thad to hurry. I was sorry we had come. This was not a good place to be.

As I had that thought, Mr. Kassel stepped out of the saloon and stood there, seemingly doing nothing other than observing the fight.

Since the last thing I wanted was for him to see me, I moved farther away, but even so, I could not keep my eyes from him. Was he the one who had taken Jacob? I think I wanted to see something that would *reveal* that he was evil. The fact is, however, that he stood there calmly, merely watching, with no visible emotion I could observe, even as the two fighters exchanged ferocious blows.

Then I was struck with the thought: *Is that what sin is, when people merely watch evil and do nothing to curb it?*

Next moment, Kassel turned and looked in my direction. In the instant, I was sure his face showed recognition. And anger. Worse, next moment, he spun about and, moving fast, rushed back inside the Mercury.

I was not sure what to do: try to go after Kassel or wait for Thad. I felt the need to tell Sam what had happened, that Mr. Kassel had seen me.

Next moment Thad reappeared on the edge of the crowd of miners. He looked around in search of me.

"Thad!" I called from across the wharf, lifting my hand. "Here."

He worked his way through the crowd. When he got close, I grabbed his arm and began to lead him away.

I said, "That Mr. Kassel came out. He saw me."

"You say anything? Did he?"

"No. Did you see Sam?"

"Gave him the lantern. Told him what we did. That we're going back early morning." Thad halted. "Think you should tell Sam that Kassel saw you?"

I shook my head. Oh, how I wished I had not come.

"I could go back, tell him," said Thad.

I looked around. The fight in front of the Mercury was still going on, with even more men watching than before. "Not sure you can," I said. "Anyway, what if that man *is* observing Sam? If you went back, he might guess you're connected."

"You decide," said Thad.

"In the morning," I said. "After we do some more searching, I'll go to his tent. Tell him."

"Ayuh. Best get away," he said.

Two days before, I'd loved California. Now I hated it.

In the darkness, we started uphill. I kept thinking about what had just happened, the brawling, Mr. Kassel, Sam and Jacob, how many ships there were, how endless, how hard our search might be. I didn't usually pray much, but I did then. "Please God," I murmured, "help me."

I had no idea what Thad was thinking because we didn't talk until we got to my tent. When we got there, all he said was "Be down early."

"Thank you."

He started off. "Good night."

"Thad," I called. "*Truly.* I appreciate your help."

"Nothing. And don't worry. We're going to find him. We will." In moments, he was out of sight.

I gazed after Thad for a few moments, thinking how lucky I was to have him for a friend. Then I ducked into our tent, which was darker than outside, stuffy and close. I felt for my bed, threw myself on it, and lay there, muscles sore, spirits jangled. I fumbled about until I found Mother's shawl and wrapped it round myself, seeking some comfort. I was hungry too, not having eaten since morning. I reminded myself how much I had wished to be a heroine. That was stupid. I just wanted to find Jacob.

Jacob is somewhere, I kept telling myself. *I have to find where. Have to.*

Like a waking nightmare, I gave myself over to remembering dangling from the ship in the dark. *That wasn't good,* I allowed myself to think. *Scary.*

I spoke into the night: "Thank you, Thad. Thank you, Sam. Thank you, Señor Rosales."

Weary, I fell asleep. My last thought before I did was: *What if I can't find Jacob? What if I really am no more than a little lamb?*

And the lobos are about.

·30·

I SLEPT POORLY, AND ROSE INTO WHAT WAS YET night. My muscles ached, my hands were stiff, my arms sore. My chest seemed heavy, and my hair felt like seaweed.

Doubts tumbled in. *I should never have come here. I should never have left Jacob alone. I'll never find him. I can't do this. I made things worse for Sam. I don't know what I'm doing. Sam, Thad, Señor Rosales, they're all doing things for me. What do I do for them? Make everything worse. And Father will be here soon. Maybe Mother. How will I be able to tell them that Jacob is gone? I hate myself.*

No! I fairly shouted at myself. *You're just making excuses.*

I scrabbled about our tent and found a cooked potato. Unsteady from tension, dissatisfied with myself, cold, wishing only to resume the search, I wrapped Mother's shawl about my shoulders and went outside.

I sat before the tent and ate the potato. I kept wishing Thad would hurry, but was not sure when he'd show up. I could see no stars or moon, the darkness made heavy by a mist that swirled around me like a wet black cloth. A briny sea-smell was strong. The smell of the city equally so. The only sound was my own uneasy breathing. Now and again I'd pass a hand over my cheeks, wiping away driblets of water. I preferred to think it was mist, not tears. I suspect I was wrong.

I shivered, drew my shawl tighter, and wished I had hot coffee. But Señor Rosales's café was not yet open, and I had no energy to make a fire. Instead, I used my flint to light my lantern. It offered a poky point of light and a hint of heat. I kept it close.

As I continued to sit there—in the middle of what seemed like a world of *nothingness*—my thoughts were mostly about Jacob. I tried to imagine where he was but was unable to summon a picture. I worried again about Sam, fearful that by my talking to the police chief, being at the Mercury, and being seen, I had put him and his father at greater risk than they already were.

I remembered something I once read: "Night is the devil's way of making you feel alone."

I kept staring uphill, looking for Thad. It was, however,

from the direction of Portsmouth Square that someone appeared out of the haze, as if materializing from a cloud. It took a moment for me to realize it wasn't Thad but a man I didn't recognize. He seemed surprised to see me too, because he halted, gawped a moment, then swerved in haste and hurried downhill, never looking back.

I watched him go, thinking I knew him. But he had shown up and disappeared so quickly I could not recall exactly where or when I'd seen him.

I looked across the way at the San Francisco Café Restaurant, and my thoughts went to Señor Rosales. Since we had said we must talk this morning, I felt obliged to tell him what I was doing lest he worry. But there was no sign of wakefulness in his café. As I was thinking of him, I saw someone coming down the hill with what looked like a fuzzy star.

It was Thad, stepping out of the mist like a scarecrow's ghost. I had told Jacob he wasn't my sweetheart. To be honest, I wasn't sure what having a sweetheart meant. All the same, I was surprised how relieved and glad I was to see him.

"Mornin'," he called.

"Good morning," I returned, standing up. "Thank you for coming."

He bobbed a nod. "Waiting long?"

"Didn't sleep well." For a moment, he and I stood face-to-face, awkward, unable to find words.

I was learning one must listen hard since what is truly said might well be mute. I had not listened well enough to Jacob. Now, as I stood there with Thad, what I felt beyond all else was gratitude. But all I said was "I have my flint case in my money belt. In case our lanterns go out again."

"Knife?"

"Always."

He wiped the wetness from his face. "Guess we better get. I'm betting we find him."

I tried to imitate his "yes" by saying "Ayuh." It came out as "Uh."

In return he gave a mocking snort.

I grinned.

I looked to the café, but there was still no sign of Señor Rosales. I said, "Let's go."

Thad and I headed downhill, lanterns held before us, splashing through muck and mud. The fog was so intense that we were unable to see more than two feet ahead. It was as if we were passing through a cloud.

Thad, echoing my thoughts, said, "Fog'll make looking harder."

"It'll lift," I said, determined to be optimistic. Moments later I tripped over something—I had no idea what—and went sprawling. Thad helped me get up, but I was damp, filthy, and distraught. My lantern had also gone out.

"You all right?"

"Fine," I said, although nothing seemed right.

He said, "My light will work."

While I worked to scrape off the mud, we kept on with Thad's lamp as I told myself I mustn't let him see my tears. I don't know if he did, but he said nothing.

We crossed over Montgomery Street and reached the cove beach but knew it only because our feet crunched in sand and I could hear the gentle *slip-slap* of water plucking against the shore. The swirling gloom made it hard to see. Even though I knew that before us, right offshore, were hundreds of Rotten Row ships, I couldn't see one of them. How do you search for what is invisible?

Thad said the obvious: "Hard to see."

I said, "We'll just row out. Can't avoid the ships. Besides," I added, "it's not as if we know where to look anyway."

Thad grunted his agreement, then led the way to where we had left our rowboat. As we approached, I saw a blob of light. Thinking of that man who'd gone past me as I waited for Thad, I halted. "Someone's there," I said.

"Hoot to a holler," said Thad, "it's Sam."

He was right. Sam had remembered where our rowboat was from the day before and was sitting in it. I was so glad to see him. A small light was at his feet, giving a glow to his face. It occurred to me that I had never seen him smile.

As we approached, he stood up. "Morning."

"Good morning," I returned. "Thanks for coming." The three of us stood staring out into the dark bay. None of us spoke. I sensed something was wrong.

Even as Sam continued to eye the bay, he said, "Kassel saw you at the Mercury last night. Told my father and me to get out. Said we can't work there anymore."

"Oh, Sam," I cried. "That's awful."

"Didn't even pay us what he owed us."

Terribly upset, I said, "We shouldn't have been there."

"Wasn't you. You were just bringing that lantern back."

"God-awful man," said Thad.

Sam finally turned around to face us. "Not saying otherwise," he said.

I said, "But . . . what will you and your father do? Can you find another job?"

"Probably, at another saloon. The saloons like music. Don't know why. Nobody listens." He sounded so sad.

"I like your playing," I said. Soon as I spoke, I felt embarrassed for offering such an empty phrase.

"My father said he might try and find us a job on a ship going back. But as I told you: risky for colored folks. Hard to know who to trust."

Thad said, "How much will it take for you to get back home?"

"Four, five hundred dollars."

Thad said, "If I get lucky at the tables, you can have it."

"Sounds good," said Sam, but not as if he thought he'd ever get the money.

"Sam . . ." I said.

"What?"

I hated the way he was treated but didn't want to say it so blandly. It seemed empty and made me tongue-tied. What I finally said was "I'm sorry for what happened."

He studied me for a few moments. At length he took a deep breath and added, "Just so you understand: When my brother vanished, we didn't know what to do. By the time we figured out what happened, he was gone. Nothing we could prove. Maybe he's on a ship. Maybe he's a slave somewhere. Maybe he got back to Sag Harbor. Hope so. We've never heard. So I'm willing to help find your brother, mostly my way of getting back at Kassel."

The three of us stood there, awkwardly, until Sam said, "OK. Your brother. You have any idea how you going to look?"

I said, "Are you sure you want . . . ?"

There was anger in his voice when he said, "I just said: finding your brother is hitting Kassel. Come on, I need to *do* something."

Somewhat abashed, I said, "I don't know a better way than to just get on some boat and search." I looked to Thad.

"Fine with me."

To Sam I said, "You have a better idea?"

"Nope," he said, and stepped out of the rowboat.

As I looked at the two boys, my emotions swelled, feeling as I did the strength of such friends. Impulsively, I went up to Sam and hugged him, then turned and did the same to Thad. Neither of them said or did anything. They were too surprised. Or maybe they were just boys. I stood back, embarrassed at my own emotions but glad I had shown them. All I could think to say was "Let's find Jacob."

·31·

I USED MY FLINT TO RELIGHT THE LANTERN, SO
now we had three glowing, which was abundant light.
Once I took off my shawl and flung it into the rowboat, it took
just moments for us to push into the cove water. I took the
center seat, placed my relit lantern at my feet, and snatched up
the oars. Thad was at the stern, his lantern next to him. Sam
was in the bow, holding his lantern high, searching for a boat.
I started rowing. "Just tell me which direction to go."

"Ahead," said Sam.

There is, I thought, *no other way to go.*

The morning fog was thicker over the bay than on land, so
dense we quickly lost sight of the beach. We could have been
a few yards from shore or a hundred miles out, on the way to

nowhere. It was only the splash of the oars and the swaying of the boat that told me that we were *on* water.

"Port," said Sam. Then after a bit, he said, "You're fine on the bow."

Thad said, "You know sailing lingo."

"Told you," returned Sam, "I come from Sag Harbor. You sail before you walk."

"A whaling port, isn't it?" Thad asked. "You ever go whaling?"

"Three-year voyage. That was enough. But I learned ships. And one of the jack tars taught me bugling."

I pulled along for a while, with no talk other than Sam's directions. "There's a ship, right—" Sam said. But suddenly he hissed, "Stop!"

Startled, I shoved the oar handles down so that the blades lifted from the water.

"No talk," Sam whispered urgently.

I listened. I heard nothing save our dripping oars: *plip-plop—plip-plop*.

"Blow the lanterns," Sam said in a low voice.

We snuffed our lights. With darkness complete, every sense of direction vanished, leaving nothing but damp air and water. I wanted to say, "What is it?" but didn't dare speak.

We drifted, the slap of water against our little boat the sole sound. Then, from somewhere—I wasn't sure from what direction—I heard what sounded like the soft splash of careful oars. It started. It stopped. Started again. I looked to where I thought the noise came from. Next moment I saw a splodge of light that lasted seconds. Everything became dark again. But something was out there.

"What was that?" I whispered. No one replied.

I listened hard, but nothing else came.

Sam, low voiced, said, "Abeam. Starboard side."

We coasted, our rowboat gently rocked by small ripples, ripples perhaps made by whoever was near—if it was someone. I tried to aim my eyes where I had seen that light, not certain if it had been truly there. The faint splashing was altogether gone.

We floated on.

I said, "*Was* it . . . someone?"

Sam, his voice still low, said, "Gone now."

"Who do you think . . . ?"

"Somebody may have seen our lantern light," said Thad. "Moved away."

Sam said, "The crimps, maybe."

"Crimps!" I cried.

"Shhh," Sam cautioned.

We didn't speak. All was still.

"Or fishermen," said Thad, keeping his voice low.

I said, "Could it have been Jacob being taken somewhere?"

"Sure . . ." muttered Sam.

Unable to restrain myself, I yelled, "Jacob!"

As if in response, I heard quick splashes on the starboard side, which made my heart thump. "Jacob!" I cried again.

Only silence.

"Dang," said Thad. "They were close."

"Took off," said Sam severely, barely above a whisper.

To me, Thad said, "You chased them off."

I felt abashed and knew I owned it. I wished I hadn't shouted.

No one spoke until I said, "How many people do you think there were?"

"No notion."

"Jacob?"

"Maybe."

"But—"

"Shhh," Sam warned. "They could be following us. They'd as soon dump and drown us as anything. Killers."

We sat in silence, our rowboat floating gently, even as my heart pounded.

I realized that the darkness had gradually turned somewhat lighter, becoming a shade of gray, enough to suggest that dawn was coming. As the night continued to lift, the dead ships seemed to rise out of the water, as if slowly emerging up from the cove water. It was fantastical.

As for another small boat, I saw none.

After a while Sam said, "When you came to the cove, anyone see you coming down the hill? Follow you?"

I thought a bit, and that's when I remembered who that man was that came upon me when I was waiting by our tent for Thad: the man with the broken nose and the pistol sitting outside the police chief's office. "A man," I said, "who knows me. Somebody who overheard what I said to the police chief."

"What did he hear?" said Sam.

"Everything you told me." Then I added, "And Señor Rosales said the police worked with the crimps. You think that's true?"

"Could be," said Thad.

I said, "Then that man knows I'm looking for Jacob."

Sam said, "Kassel saw you at the Mercury last night. And that man you saw, if your señor is right, I'd say he and Kassel are working together to keep you from your brother."

Thad said, "Maybe the one we just heard out here."

The thought of that violent-looking man made my nervousness increase. I said, "Do you think he came about and is following us?"

No one answered. Just listened. In the hush that followed, all I could hear were my own rebuking thoughts: *Stupid, stupid.*

After a while, Sam said, "All right, then, understand: if the police *are* working with Kassel and they know you're looking for your brother, it'll make things worse. Boots to buttons, they're out here, either dodging us or trying to find us."

"Which?"

"Take your pick."

Thad stared out over the water. "Whoever they are, they're gone. We better move."

"But," I asked, "what if they are following us?"

Sam said, "Hey, we either do something or not."

"Anyway," added Thad, "can't be sure it was them. Just need to keep listening."

I began to row again, trying to make as little noise as possible. There was just enough light so we didn't have to relight the lanterns.

No one spoke until Sam said, "Ahead—there's a ship."

There was a thump. Our rowboat jolted.

"We're on her," said Thad.

·32·

I'LL LOOK FOR A WAY TO GET ON," I SAID, AND began to row round the ship's hull, looking for a rope ladder. On the stern I could read the ship's name, *Western Queen*.

Sam, in the bow, held up his lantern. "Got something," he called. He grabbed a limp line and tied it to our rowboat.

Next moment, he scrambled up the side of the ship, going much faster than Thad and I had done. He even had his lamp handle looped about his arm.

Thad followed, then me, climbing the way we had before, which might best be described as crawling up the hull. It was hard, though this ship proved easier than the one the night before. I was becoming practiced.

It wasn't long before all three of us were standing on the main deck.

To Sam, Thad said, "Where'd you learn to climb like that?"

"On the whaler. Climb enough masts and spars, you climb anything."

"How old were you?"

"Seven."

"Young."

"Told you: some people like to be waited on."

We looked about. A blanket of gray mist blurred everything while a whiff of decay hung over all. Even so, we could see that the *Western Queen* was enormous, much bigger than the two ships Thad and I had been on the night before. It gave forth soft grindings and creaking, the noise coming from everywhere and nowhere all at once. The *Western Queen* may have been in her watery grave, but she lay uneasy.

Another large ship floated right next to her, so near that spars from both ships wove among one another, like interlinked fingers.

"Tory," Thad called, "let me have your flint box."

One by one he relit our three lanterns.

The three of us stayed close, wandering around the deck, trying not to make noise but peering into everything.

"See that?" said Sam. He pointed to what looked like a big brick box sitting on the deck. "It's a tryworks, which means we're on a whaler. It's where they boil down the blubber. Right now, in our lanterns, we could be burning the oil they made."

Sam, with his superior knowledge of ships, led the way, and enabled us to search effectively. It made no difference. We found no hint of Jacob.

After coming onto a companionway, Sam guided us down to the tween deck. It was all a jumble: a mix of clothing, open trunks, crockery, hats, shoes, lamps, and bedding, as if the crew had left the ship in great haste, perhaps right after dropping their anchor into the cove, just as I had witnessed on the *Stephanie K.*

Every time we opened a door or looked into a cabin, I'd become tense, hoping we were about to find Jacob. It must have been obvious because Sam turned to me and said, "Want some advice?"

"Please."

"Not easy," he said. "But don't go expecting to find your brother every turn we take. You'll get so twitchety, you'll give yourself brain-hurt. We find him, good. Otherwise, we'll just keep looking."

And look we did. Using our rowboat, we went to perhaps seven ships, if not more. I lost count. Each boat was a bit different — two masts or three; fancy woodwork or dull woodwork; steering wheel, rudder bar, steering house, or steering well — yet they seemed much the same. Main decks. Companionways. Tween decks. Cargo hold.

The more we searched, the faster we went, clambering from ship to ship.

After boarding yet another ship, a large three-masted vessel, we hurried over the main deck but found nothing. Then we went into the galley, where plates, some with rotten food, lay on a long table. Much of it had been eaten by rats. Their droppings were everywhere.

"Might as well try the forecastle before moving on," said Sam. Holding the lantern before him, he took us along the lower deck, toward the bow. The forecastle, Sam explained, was where ordinary crew members had their living quarters. We reached it, found the door open, and went in.

It was an extended cabin, shaped like a half-moon. On the long, straight, middle side was what looked to be a mast running from below and up through the ceiling. On the port side, which was curved, our lantern light revealed two levels of deep bunk beds, eight in all, some with bedding. There were sea chests on the floor, clothing hanging on pegs.

On the starboard side was a fixed table, with two bowls and as many spoons. It was as though someone had just been eating and had left only moments ago.

It was I who saw the copper-colored coin. It lay next to one of the half-empty plates. I picked it up. When I looked at it closely, I gasped.

·33·

WHAT IS IT?" SAID SAM.

"My brother's Henry Clay token."

"Token?"

"Something my father gave Jacob. From an election. My brother always had it with him." I looked at the others. "He must have been just here. Eating at this table."

"Gorry," cried Thad. "That boat we heard."

"Taking him somewhere else," said Sam.

With the token in my fist, I tore away and bolted up the companionway, back to the main deck. Once there, I rushed to the topgallant rail—one side and then the other—and stared out into the ashen dawn as if somehow I might see Jacob. All I saw were the massive hulks of nearby ships.

Thad and Sam found me at the rail. I was still gazing outward, tense with distress, trying to keep my pain within. I was also clutching that token as if it were Jacob.

"Anything?" asked Thad.

"Jacob *was* here," I said. "That man who saw me, he guessed we'd be coming to search for him. When we went one way, he went another and took Jacob. It just happened."

Sam said, "Didn't need to be us coming to make them move him."

Thad added, "Might've been their plan all along."

"I just want to know *where* they took him," I said.

"Another ship," said Thad.

"I know that," I cried out in exasperation. "But which one?"

"What I told you," said Sam. "If they just took him, most likely they've brought him to a ship that's about to leave the bay. That's the way crimpers work."

"Then . . . what ships are going?" I asked, willing to grasp at anything that could be helpful. "Can we find out?"

Thad said, "They post the names of ships about to leave at my store."

"Then go and get their names," I said, as if giving an order. Realizing how harsh I must have sounded, I added, "Would you, please?"

Thad gave me a look, as if to say "Go easy," but all he said was "Sure."

"Sam," I said, "will you keep searching with me? Maybe we'll be lucky. Do you have time?"

"I'm not working."

"Oh, Sam . . . I forgot."

He lifted a shoulder.

Thad said, "Somebody has to row me to shore."

Full of new resolve, I said, "Let's go."

We hurried off the ship and back into the rowboat. Thad was in the bow, Sam in the stern, me in the middle at the oars. I rowed back to the beach, so hard my hands hurt. Soon as we got close enough, Thad, holding his lantern, jumped out and waded to shore.

"How you going to know when to pick me up?" he called from the beach.

"It's getting lighter," said Sam. "We'll see you. Or wave your lantern."

To which I added, "If we don't come, shout."

I watched Thad walk along the beach until he became lost in the grayness, though his flickering lantern, like a firefly, remained in sight a longer while.

Using one oar, I spun the rowboat about.

Sam said, "I can row faster."

I gave way, and Sam, standing, took up the oars and began to work them. I went to the bow. The morning air was cold and clammy.

Trembling from chill and tension, I put my shawl around me and pulled it tight. Adding to my frustration, the dawn's light dimmed as dense fog returned. Sam, still standing, rowed hard. The cove beach rapidly vanished from view.

I said, "Why do you row standing?"

"Sag Harbor way."

In the bow, I held up my lantern. "Hard to see," I said as we headed out.

"A few weeks ago," said Sam, "a ship coming in had to stay outside the Gate for seven days, waiting for the fog to clear."

"When my family came, it was five days."

"Might have a good side."

"What?"

"The fog keeps ships out, but it also locks them in. Might mean the ship your brother's on can't sail. Could give us extra time."

When we got in among the Rotten Row ships, Sam shipped the oars and held up his lantern. I held mine up as well. When I gazed up at the neglected ships, all I saw was a tangle of gigantic hulls, masts, and spars, all fading into the fog. It made me think of a vast spiderweb, and that Jacob was caught in it, somewhere. The notion put goose bumps on my arm.

I pulled my shawl around me tighter.

Sam said, "Any notion as to which boat you want to search?"

I looked about. "No idea."

"Hate to tell you," said Sam, "be mostly luck."

"Let's try that one," I said, pointing to the nearest ship.

We got on her the way we had the others. As before, Sam was a lot faster climbing up the hull, but I was getting better.

We searched the deck, looked down hatchways, called and called again. We found nothing.

As the dawn grew brighter, our searching became easier. And with ships in this area pressed so close, we could jump from one to another and didn't have to return to the rowboat. That saved time.

We searched five ships: main decks, twin decks, forecastles. We even checked deep holds, with me constantly calling for Jacob. We found no trace.

We decided to go back to our rowboat and go to another part of Rotten Row. That we did. We found a ship — our sixth one — that had a rope ladder, and climbed on board. As Sam began to look about, I, feeling discouraged, held back. I stood on the main deck and looked toward shore, hoping I'd see or hear Thad. Our search would be so much easier if we learned which ships were leaving. That is, if we could find them.

Wishing Thad would hurry, I remained in place, listening hard. The eddying fog had thickened, so I couldn't see shore or city. But, as I stood there, I heard what sounded like the soft splash-splash of oars.

"Thad?" I shouted, thinking that maybe he was coming after us on his own.

At my call, the rowing sounds ceased abruptly. I waited. All I heard was what sounded like the wash of water.

I remembered that police officer. *What if he's been following us all along and that was his oar sounds? Means he knows where we are.*

I whirled about. "Sam!" I called. "Come here and listen. Quick."

When Sam didn't reply, I assumed he had gone to the lower deck. I hurried over and looked down the companion-way.

"Sam!" I cried.

No answer.

I tied my shawl round my waist in a tighter knot and hurried down the steep steps, holding on with two hands. It was much darker below, making it hard to see.

"Sam!"

"Here!"

It took some moments for me to find him on the tween deck.

I said, "I may have heard someone. It could be Thad trying to find us. Or someone else. Come up and listen."

Sam said, "Let me just check in here."

He was moving toward the forecastle. I followed. There

was just enough light for us to see that the door was closed with a metal hasp lock—an iron peg on a cord. Sam undid it with ease and pulled the door open. We went in and looked about.

It was a long and narrow space, quite dark, with one small porthole, which let in some little light. That allowed for some fresh air, a good thing because the area was close and fetid, the smell of rot intense. I said, "Did you live on ship in places like this?"

"'Course."

We started to examine the empty crew berths.

A noise came from overhead.

The instant we heard it, we stood still, looked up, and listened. The sounds weren't the moans and rasping of ship timbers we'd grown used to. These were sharp and hard.

Sam pointed toward the ceiling and mouthed the word: *Footsteps.*

"Thad?"

"Don't know."

I listened fixedly. "Just now," I whispered, "on deck, I heard something out in the water."

Sam said, "This ship has a ladder. Easy to get on."

More sounds.

After a few moments, Sam, in a low voice, said, "One person. Don't move."

I didn't.

The overhead footsteps halted, resumed, and then grew quiet. We waited there, in the forecastle's semidarkness, intent on sounds. At some point, I realized I was observing a feeble light through the open door. I stared at it. Though ill defined, it appeared to be someone holding a lantern.

"Thad!" I called.

"Shhh," Sam hissed sharply.

The outside person not only ceased to move but made no reply. Then the light vanished.

"Not Thad," Sam whispered.

I took a step forward only to have Sam grab my arm and hold me back. "Careful. He's blocking the door."

Sam made a waving motion. I took it to mean I was to move to one side of the door, which I did. He went to the other side. I understood: if someone came forward into the forecastle, we could slip behind him and get out.

Again, we waited.

Next moment, there was a *slamming* sound. The door had been shut. On the instant, Sam threw himself against it and pulled. It was of no use. We were locked in.

·34·

WHAT WE HEARD NEXT WAS THE SOUND OF running steps. Whoever had shut the door was sprinting away, the footfalls diminishing fast. Then all became silent.

Sam went to the door. He fumbled for the latch, then shook and rattled it. It refused to budge. "Locked," he said. "We were dumb to stay in here."

"Did you see who it was?"

"No."

I joined Sam. The two of us struggled with the door. It wouldn't open.

"He probably pegged the hasp," said Sam.

I pulled out my knife and used it to poke at the door. That proved useless.

I heard Sam's agitated breathing.

"Who," I said, "do you think it was?"

"You just heard someone out on the water, didn't you?"

"Think so."

"That crimp. He did follow you." He was looking around. "We're stuck. At least we have air." He gestured toward the small porthole.

"Thad will come," I said.

"With all these dead ships," said Sam, "how's he going to figure out which one we're on?" There was anger in his voice.

I envisioned Thad on the beach, calling to us, we not responding. I said, "He'll know *something* happened. Come after us."

"Maybe."

Sam was right, though: even if Thad guessed things had gone amiss, he'd have no idea where we were.

Out of heart, blaming myself for shouting, I sat on the floor, and with my back propped against a wall, tried to think what to do. I had no ideas. Cold, I reached for my shawl, only to realize it must have fallen off. I didn't even bother to look for it. The damp clung to me. I shivered.

"I make a lot of mistakes," I said.

"People do," returned Sam. He was sitting against a nearby wall.

For the longest while we didn't speak. Twice, we attempted to force the door. It was of no use.

After a while, I said, "Sam, what's going to happen to us?"

"Nothing."

"But—"

"Told you, Kassel don't give a hoot. You think that crimper cares? Took my brother, didn't they? Took yours. Why should they worry about us?" He was quiet for a moment and then said, "What about your friend, Señor Rosales? Does he have any idea where we are?"

"Not . . . really. Does . . . your father know?"

"Didn't tell him I was coming here. Wouldn't have let me."

"Why?"

"He told me to have nothing to do with Kassel. Or you. The only thing he can think about is trying to find work so as to get us back east."

"By ship?"

"Don't think walking will work."

We lapsed into silence.

"Sam . . . we can't stay here forever."

"Forever is not going to happen."

"What do you mean?"

"We'll either die here—starve—or they'll come and do away with us."

"Why?"

"They got a good business going."

"But . . . but I don't *want* to be here," I cried out, only to realize how pointless it was to act and say such things that way. As I sat there I recalled believing—when my family sailed into San Francisco—that life was enhanced when embracing danger. *Childish*, I told myself.

Sam remained quiet.

I continued to sit, though at one point I shouted out, "Thad!" It was yet another useless thing to do.

Sam said nothing.

We sat, waited, and listened to the sounds of the old ship creaking. I'm not sure how long we were there, but at some point, I had an idea. "My shawl," I said.

"What about it?"

"I dropped it. I think in here somewhere."

"You cold?"

"That small porthole. If I dangle the shawl out and Thad sees it, he might guess where we are."

It took some time, but we found the shawl on one of the berths. It took only a moment for me to push it out through the small porthole so that most of it hung outside. From that point on, all we could do was wait, and hope.

The air was cold and clammy, as if the fog had seeped in and closed around us. In the dimness, it was impossible to say how much time passed. We didn't talk much. And, as I had eaten hardly anything that day, my hunger increased.

At some point, I began to hear high-pitched squeaking.

"Rats," Sam said. "If they get close, kick at them."

I hugged myself that much tighter.

To keep up my spirits, I asked Sam to tell me about his time on a whaling ship. His tales about his three-year voyage were extraordinary.

In return, he asked me about my life. To my ears, our family existence in Providence was altogether indifferent. But when I told him why and how we came to California, our accounts were not so unlike: our fathers' fever for gold.

"You sorry you came to California?" he asked.

"Most of it was good," I said, "until Jacob. . . . You sorry?"

"Yup. My father and I, all we want to do is to get home to Sag Harbor, safe and free." After a while he asked, "You think your father will get lots of gold?"

"Be splendid if he did. But . . . I don't think he will."

"Why?"

"You know: not many do. And it's not his kind of work."

"If he did get gold, what would he do with it?"

"He's going build us a big house. What's your home—back east—like?"

Sam described his village as a small fishing and whaling port on Long Island, about a hundred miles from New York City.

I said, "If my father gets gold, I'll make him buy you passage home."

"Thanks," said Sam. "But you just said you didn't think he'll get much."

"True."

We lapsed into dreary silence.

After a while, I said, "Tell me about your brother."

Sam held off a bit, then said, "Named Otis. When I was little, I couldn't say it right. Called him Oats. It stuck. Older than me. Smart. A fiddler. Good one too. Oats was my best—"

Even as Sam spoke, we heard the unmistakable sounds of steps overhead again.

"Shhh," Sam cautioned.

We stared up. The steps kept on, slow, careful.

"It might be Thad," I whispered. "I could call."

"Like last time? What if it's the crimps coming to finish us?"

I shut my mouth.

The footsteps crossed overhead, faded, and then died out. Within moments, they resumed. Whoever was on the main deck appeared to be wandering. Perhaps searching. I could only hope the person didn't discover where we were.

Next moment, I told myself that the crimps had locked us in here, so these footsteps couldn't be made by the same people. That is, unless they were coming to make sure we were still here and were intending to do away with us.

The footsteps ceased, as if the person above were gone. We

remained motionless. Moments later, however, a faint light—shaped like the blade of a white knife—poked under the forecastle door, into where we were. It was all too clear: whoever had been above was now on the lower deck, not far from where we were.

As I stared at the light, it appeared to be growing brighter. The person was approaching the door.

In the faint glow, I saw Sam make a motion. It was as he had suggested before: I should move to the right side of the door, while he went to the left. If the person opened the door—and intended to do us harm—we might be able to get out or overpower whoever it was.

In quiet haste, we took our positions and stood, waiting. I tried to keep calm. But I took out my knife and held it in my hand.

The light withdrew.

I heard someone fumbling with the latch. The door began to swing open.

I held my breath.

·35·

"TORY? SAM? YOU IN HERE?"

"Thad!" I cried.

The door was pulled open, and there stood Thad, lit lantern in hand. "What the dickens you two doing in here?"

Though I could have sworn he was smirking, never in all my life was I so glad to see anyone. I flung myself at him and gave him a hug. As for Sam, I saw him grin. The first time.

In a great rush, I told Thad what had happened.

He said, "Any idea who locked you in?"

"Has to be the crimps," said Sam. "How'd you find us?"

"Soon as I checked the list of outgoing ships at my store, I came back to the beach and started hollering. When you didn't come, I figured something had happened. Got me a boat and rowed around. Took a while, but then I saw Tory's red shawl drooping from this here ship. Not hard after that. Glad I found you."

Thank you, Mother, I thought. But what I said was, "Let's get off this boat."

We all but ran up to the main deck, then scrambled down the rope ladder, but I didn't feel safe until I was in Thad's row-boat. Once there, with him at the oars, we began to move away from the hulk in which we had been trapped.

"What time is it?" I asked.

Thad said, "'Bout noon."

"What's the date?"

"Near end of November."

Almost December. December was when my father had promised to return. My heart hurt.

The fog was thin, and the day had become warmer. We rowed about in search of the rowboat Sam and I had left behind. When we found it, we towed her along as we headed back to shore. It was only then that I said to Thad, "Did you find out which ships are leaving?"

"Only one that's been cleared, the *Yankee Sword,* was for today. But changed for tomorrow. Don't know why."

"Fog," said Sam.

Thad said, "She's headed for Panama."

I remembered: that was the one Jacob talked of joining. What if he had? No. Impossible.

Sam said, "If she's heading there, it means she's going to pick up new immigrants. Which also means when she goes, she'll be mostly empty."

"Could Jacob be on her?" I asked.

Thad said, "She's the first one going out, isn't she?"

I said, "Jacob told me they were looking for a cabin boy."

"There you are," said Sam.

"Think he could be on her *now*?"

Thad said, "We're pretty sure they just moved him, didn't they? Probably why they locked you up."

Sam said, "Can't be sure he's there, but we should look."

I said, "Could we get on her? Search?"

"You can't just board her," said Sam. "And if he's there, they'll never let you on."

As soon as our boat touched the beach, we climbed out. The fog was gone, replaced by dreary drizzle.

I turned to Sam. "Do you need to tell your father what's happened?"

"If I do, he won't let me out of the tent."

Thad said, "We sure need you."

"Told you," said Sam. "I'm not doing it for you. My way of going against Kassel."

"I'm grateful," I said, and reached out and held his arm, and gave it a little shake. "We couldn't do this without you."

Sam didn't pull away. All he said was "I know."

I said, "I need to speak to Señor Rosales. I promised to tell him what I'm doing."

Thad said, "What *are* you doing?"

"Not sure," I returned, feeling exasperated. "But I need to speak to him."

"Where's your friend?" asked Sam.

"Up the hill."

"Let's go," said Sam, and the three of us started off.

Though I had no idea what the boys were thinking, for my part, I wanted to believe that Jacob was being held on the *Yankee Sword*. The notion both encouraged me *and* scared me. Encouraged that we had a real idea where he might be. Scared that if the ship *was* about to leave, we had to get to her fast. At the same time, I had to acknowledge what Sam had said: we weren't truly sure Jacob *was* on her. And even if he was, we had no notion how we could get him off.

My worry led me to a further thought: that Señor Rosales just might be wrong, that perhaps that man I'd seen in the police office — the one with the broken nose — had acted on his own. That made me think that if I told Chief Fallon what had happened to us — being trapped on that ship — he'd know that Jacob was in trouble and he'd help. It would make things so much easier. Surely, *he* could board the *Yankee Sword*.

Fortified by the idea, I moved faster. Thad and Sam stayed with me.

We never reached our tent. Señor Rosales saw us coming and ran out from his café. "¡Hola!" he cried. "Corderita, I'm glad to see you. Any news of Jacob?"

"We think so. This is Sam. He's been helping us look."

"Mucho gusto," said Señor Rosales, shaking Sam's hand, but he was more intent on my account of all that had happened.

"Good for you," he said to Sam when I was done. "And you too," he said to Thad, "for helping Tory."

I said, "Señor Rosales, I want to go back to Chief Fallon."

He grimaced. "Señorita, I told you, he may be working with these crimps."

"We don't know that for certain."

Señor Rosales looked to Sam and Thad as if to get them to convince me.

"If Fallon is connected to the crimps," Thad reminded me, "and you go to him, you'll only be telling them we're off that ship."

"Won't be good," Sam agreed.

"I know it's risky," I said, "but he could make a big difference. I have to try." Not wishing to wait a moment more, and without lingering to see if my friends would join me, I started off for Portsmouth Square. The others, albeit reluctantly, followed.

I approached the square from the south side. As ever, it was swarming with men. I worked through the crowds, but as soon as I spied the old schoolhouse — the police office — I came to a halt. Four men were standing in front of the building, talking. I recognized three of them: Chief Fallon, Mr. Kassel, and the man with the broken nose.

I needed no further proof: Chief Fallon was working with the crimpers.

My friends came up to where I was standing. "What's the matter?" asked Sam.

I pointed. "The police house. See those men."

"Ugly," said Sam.

"Who's the fourth one?" I asked. He was a large man, with a shock of white hair and a large white beard.

"Captain Littlefield," said Thad. "I've seen him about our store, buying supplies. Guess what? He's captain of the *Yankee Sword*."

"That's all the proof I need," I cried. "Why else would he be with those people? Jacob *must* be on her."

Sam started to back away, pulling me with him. "Be better if they don't see us. Let 'em think we're still locked up on that ship."

We hurried off, Señor Rosales quite puzzled. As soon as we were out of the square, I explained it to him. "You were right," I said. "The police are working with the crimps. I think that man — remember the man with the broken nose in the police house?—I think he's the one who locked up Sam and me on the ship."

"Madre de Dios," said Señor Rosales. "The policía and the crimpers. That's what I was told. When does this *Yankee Sword* depart?"

"Tomorrow, latest," said Thad.

"Santo Cristo. Have you studied this ship?"

"Not really."

"Come back to my café. Use my telescope. Maybe you'll even be able to see Jacob. That would help."

Once we got the telescope, it was Sam who said, "We'll see more from Goat Hill."

"Por favor, keep the telescope," said Señor Rosales. "But you must promise to come back and tell me what you intend to do. ¿Lo prometes? Soy responsible. You must not do anything peligroso."

Thad turned to me as we headed away. "What's peligroso mean?"

Señor Rosales had taught me well. I said, "Dangerous."

·36·

WE HURRIED, BUT GOAT HILL WAS A STEEP climb, so it was not till midafternoon that we reached the top. Directly across the bay was Angel Island. To the north of us was Alcatraces, or Pelican Island, the desolate place I'd seen when I first came into the bay. Two miles from San Francisco, it sat like a guard before the Golden Gate. As for the Golden Gate, a great gray fog bank was blocking the way, like a cotton cork stuffed in the neck of a narrow bottle.

To the east was the expanse of the great bay. That was open.

We sat down and Thad put the telescope to his eyes. It took him a moment before he said, "The *Yankee Sword* is right there. See? Sails furled. Anchored. Just beyond Rotten Row. Name in yellow letters on her stern. They're loading her."

Sam looked. Then he said, "Unless that fog bank holds her back, the *Yankee Sword* will be leaving soon. We better decide fast what we're doing."

I took the telescope and studied the ship. Being a brig, the *Yankee Sword* was not so large, with only two masts; the forward mast was taller than the main mast. Attached to that rear mast was a gaff that held a square sail over the stern. At her bow was a sprit nearly the length of the deck that extended forward over the water.

Since San Francisco had few loading docks extending into the bay—at least not as far out as the *Yankee Sword* was anchored—lighters were bringing out her cargo. As we watched, passing the telescope among us, there were decreasing numbers of lighters, suggesting that the loading was a fair way to being completed.

Sam, after looking again, said, "Not that many men on her."

I took back the telescope, hoping to catch sight of Jacob. But it didn't matter that I couldn't see him. By then I was convinced he *was* there.

We sat in silence. I didn't know what to do.

It was Thad who said, "I have an idea."

"Say it."

"All those lighters loading her, right?"

"What about them?" said Sam.

"We could get hold of one," Thad went on, "go on out to

the *Yankee Sword*, climb on board, and look around for your brother."

"In *daylight*?" said Sam.

Thad said, "They're so busy getting ready to leave that they might not notice us."

Sam shook his head. "Three kids wandering around the ship? Poking about? They'd see us soon enough. Too risky."

To which I added, "And they might catch us. Keep us. Or worse."

Thad had no reply.

After a moment, I said, "How about going to her tonight? It'll be dark. The fog might be thicker too."

Sam said, "They're sure to have a watch posted. And safety lights. If they're keeping a lookout, there we'd be, in a dinky rowboat. Won't matter it being dark. They'd see us for sure."

"But we can't wait any longer," I said. "She's scheduled to leave *tomorrow*."

There was some silence before Thad said, "Then I'm betting the best chance we have is now."

I said, "To do what?"

Thad said, "Have a closer look."

"How?"

"Grab a boat and go on out there."

I scrambled to my feet. "Come on," I said. "We need to."

It took us a while to get off the hill, but once we did,

we went right to the cove, fetched up a rowboat, and pushed it into the water. I took a place in the bow, telescope in hand. Thad was on the stern seat. Sam began to row.

No one spoke as we worked our way through the Rotten Row hulks. It took a while, but once we broke through into the bay, I looked to where the *Yankee Sword* was, only to blink at what I was *not* seeing.

The ship wasn't there.

At first I thought I wasn't looking in the right direction. I even stood up and shaded my eyes. No question: the *Yankee Sword* was not where we had last seen her. "She's gone!" I cried.

After a moment, Thad pointed and said, "No. There she is. In deeper water."

"Is she moving?"

Sam used the telescope. "No," he said.

Thad turned to Sam. "What's she doing?"

Sam continued studying her. "Looks like she finished loading. The sails are down and she's anchored, so she's staying away from shore, not going anywhere. Maybe waiting for the fog to clear from the Gate and for the tides to run right. Anyway, she won't be leaving. Not yet."

"I'm guessing," said Thad, "once all is good, she'll glide right on out."

With our rowboat gently rocking, we kept watching the *Yankee Sword* in silence.

"If we go after her in this boat," said Thad, "we'll be as obvious as turtles in a washtub."

"And," said Sam, "if they get suspicious, they might pull anchor and race off. No way could we catch her in the bay with this." He patted the gunwales of our little boat.

"But we can't do nothing," I cried.

Though no one disagreed, no one suggested anything. Our rowboat began to drift while we continued to stare at the brig.

It was Thad who said, "Tory, remember when we first went looking 'round Rotten Row—that ketch we searched?"

"What about her?"

"Sign on her said HELP YOURSELF."

"I don't know what you're saying."

"Remember? She looked ready to sail. We could get on her, go after the *Yankee Sword* in her." He turned to Sam. "Could you sail a small ketch?"

"Reckon."

I said, "If the *Yankee Sword* moved away, could a small boat like that go after her?"

"Long as she stayed in the bay," said Sam. "But . . . not if she gets to ocean."

Thad said, "They might not notice a small boat." Then he added, "Much."

The boys looked to me.

I said, "Let's go and use her."

We headed back to Rotten Row. As both Thad and I recalled, the ketch was not deeply embedded midst the Rotten Row fleet but somewhere along its outer edges. Even so, it took a while before we found her.

After all the big ships we had been on, she seemed smaller than I recalled: maybe thirty feet in length with one mainmast, plus the modest mizzenmast near the stern. The signs— OFF FOR RICHES, HELP YOURSELF—were still there. When we pulled close, I noticed her name: *Sadie Rose.* Somebody's sweetheart or wife.

We drew alongside, tied the rowboat to a loose line so it wouldn't drift off, and scrambled on board.

The full rig of sails—flying jib, staysail, fore staysail, mainsail, and mizzen—remained hanging from the masts. Lines seemed to be where they were supposed to be, albeit tangled. Strewn about were the tools I'd noticed before.

Sam stood amidships and, with his seaman's eye, appraised her.

"Can you sail her?" I asked.

"Think so."

Thus it was that Sam became captain of the *Sadie Rose,* or "Cap'n," as Thad called him with a sharp salute.

I shall not bore you with all Sam's ship language—his commands, which, in any case, he often had to translate for my landlubber's ears, as much as Señor Rosales translated his

Spanish. Enough to say, Sam put Thad and me to work. As quick as possible, the deck had been cleared, the mainsail, jib, and mizzen hauled.

"What about our rowboat?" I said.

"Tie her to our stern," said Sam. "We might need her. Just in case. Push her oars under the seat."

That done, it took the three of us to work the ketch's anchor up from where it lay embedded in bottom mud, where its twin flukes—like hooks—held fast.

I was reminded of the Rhode Island symbol: an anchor. Stay in place. *Ancora.* Hope. Hope was what I needed.

With the anchor freed and aboard, Sam turned the *Sadie Rose* downwind and away from Rotten Row. Out in the bay, the choppy waters caught at our low bow and sent wet and shivery cold salt spray over us. Now and again light rain also sprinkled. But we were moving sprightly, which gave me a sense that we really going somewhere. That made me warm.

It did require some time for Sam to gain a *feel*—as he put it—for the ketch, and for Thad and me to understand his orders so we could follow them. In good time, however, we were sailing about the bay with ease, as all three of us worked like old jacks. Our rowboat bobbed behind.

Sam maneuvered the *Sadie Rose* so that while we kept our distance from the *Yankee Sword*, we were able to keep our eyes on her. As Sam explained, he didn't want her crew to have any suspicions as to who we were or why we were out there. Besides, Señor Rosales's telescope allowed us to be watchful while keeping our distance. I was becoming excited, filled with the sense that we were truly drawing closer to Jacob.

All the while, the *Yankee Sword* remained motionless, though now and again I saw people move about her deck. I need hardly say that I saw nothing of Jacob.

As we tacked back and forth, we would turn toward the Golden Gate. That fog bank had only crept farther into the bay. It had also become thicker, darker, too, like a thundercloud.

Let me acknowledge, however, that though we were in the bay and keeping our eyes on the brig, we had yet to form a plan as to how to rescue Jacob. It was as if we were waiting for the *Yankee Sword* to tell us what to do. It was when we darted in close and Thad was studying her with his telescope that he called, "Come about!"

Sam shifted the tiller hard.

"What is it?" I asked.

"Someone was standing at her bow. I could have sworn he was looking at us."

"What's he look like?"

Thad looked again. "White hair."

I said, "Captain Littlefield."

"He'll know about us, then," said Sam, and continued to tack away from the *Yankee Sword*.

"Do we have to worry?" I asked.

"We're too far away," said Thad.

"I'm not so sure," said Sam.

By late afternoon, with sunlight fast diminishing, the *Yankee Sword* had hung lights forward and aft. Another light dangled from a midship spar.

"What do those lights mean?" I asked Sam, who had kept us at a distance.

"Safety lights," he explained. "Tells me she's not going anywhere. Not tonight. Probably hoping that the fog in the Gate lifts so they can leave early morning."

We continued to sail back and forth, in no particular direction but always keeping the *Yankee Sword* in view. Twilight brought deeper murk. What's more, the shadowy fog in the Gate was flowing into the bay, spreading, like a balloon slowly swelling bigger.

Sam said, "It's going to get too dark for us out here. If we keep sailing about, someone on that ship is bound to get suspicious."

"But we have to keep watching her," I said.

For a moment, no one spoke.

Thad said, "What about Alcatraces? That island. Sits before the Gate. If we can get on it, we can keep an eye on the ship. We have the telescope."

"Will they notice us?" I asked Sam.

"Not likely."

Thad added, "And if she tries to run for the Gate, she'll have to pass right by us."

I said, "But if she did run by, we still don't know how we'll get Jacob."

Thad said, "We'll think of something then."

"Is anybody on the island?" I asked.

"Rocks and birds," said Sam, adding, "Won't be pleasant sitting there." Then he added further, "Still . . . better than sailing about. And if we sit high up, we'll be able to see the *Yankee Sword* a whole lot better than from here." He patted the gunwales.

I said, "Then we should do it." I looked to Thad.

"Ayuh."

I turned to Sam. He responded by blowing out his cheeks as if playing his bugle, let go a puff of air, and then shifted the tiller, all he needed to do by way of saying yes.

The boom swung about. The ketch heeled. As the twilight dimmed and the fog grew murkier, the *Sadie Rose* headed for the Isle of Alcatraces.

·37·

THE ISLAND OF ALCATRACES MAY HAVE APPEARED small from the summit of Goat Hill, but it grew larger and more inhospitable the nearer we came. In the increasing dark, it appeared as little more than a mass of gray-blue rocks, all of different sizes and sharp shapes. The island made me think of a gigantic, barnacle-encrusted whale, lying dead upon the waters.

Since our boat had a keel, and the island shore being nothing but low, jagged cliffs, and with strong currents swirling about, Sam had to work hard to get the *Sadie Rose* close in. When he did, masses of birds (mostly pelicans and gulls) burst up, crowding the air with their flapping wings. Flying low, they screeched, barked, and dove at us, swooping

so close we often had to stoop. It was as if they were telling us that they alone held exclusive claim to this pile of
jagged stone.

As we drew close, our keel scrapped bottom.

"Can't get nearer," said Sam.

"The rowboat," said Thad.

Sam, to me, said, "Toss our anchor."

I scrambled forward and heaved the heavy hook, which
splashed down.

"Give it a yank," cried Sam. "Make sure it's set."

"Holding," I called.

Thad dropped our sails.

Sam pulled the rowboat close.

Thad grabbed the telescope. "We'll need this."

In mindless readiness, I checked my money belt, with its
knife.

One by one, we climbed into the rowboat, then pushed off
from the *Sadie Rose.*

Having taken the center seat, I took up the oars and rowed
as near to the island as possible. Waves and flowage pushed us
closer until Thad, impatient, leaped for shore. He landed on a
jutting rock, almost lost his balance, and saved himself by wild
winglike waving of his long arms—as if trying to outflap the
birds. It worked. He kept his footing and was safe. Then he
waded back in the water, grabbed the rowboat line, and pulled

her in. I climbed out. Sam, telescope in hand, came from the stern. We all hauled the boat up on the shore so the currents wouldn't bash her onto the rocks. That done, Sam found a stone around which to wrap her line.

United, we climbed higher onto the empty island so as to get a better view of the *Yankee Sword*. When we found a flat place, we sat side by side, gazing eastward into the bay like a trio of Crusoes.

It was now evening. A damp murkiness clung close, a blanket of dense and soggy air, whose thickness made it difficult to distinguish water from air. There were no stars, only a high and fuzzy full moon that seemed to smolder in the sky, its edgeless halo casting little light. The three lamps on the *Yankee Sword* remained in dull sight — an earthbound constellation — so we knew she was there, not going anywhere.

As we sat there, no one talking, I listened to the bay water *lip-lap* against the island rocks. Here and there the rippling water shimmered. The island birds, for the most part, had become noiseless, though now and again I heard a faint twittering, the sudden squawk of a seagull, a barking pelican, plus my own anxious breath.

"Wish I had my bugle," said Sam.

"I bet you'd play 'I Often Think of Writing Home.'"

"Probably would."

I wondered: Where was my home? Was it back in Providence? Or had San Francisco become my home?

I said, "Do you miss your home a lot?"

Sam said, "Do. Keep hoping Oats got there. Saving your brother will give me some faith."

I said, "Oh, Sam, I want your brother safe too."

"Appreciate that."

I was thinking about Sam's brother when, to the left of us, a ship emerged out of the fog, moving slowly eastward into the bay. Though I was not given to believing in worlds that go beyond God's creation, the ship appeared ghostlike, slow and silent in the murky light. Her unexpected appearance, festooned by veils of mist as much as sail, suggested that she had sailed in from another world, shaped and propelled by the air itself. Seeing her gave me an awful thought: that she was a spirit ship, coming to take Jacob away.

I hastened to scold myself, knowing that, of course, the ship was real and must have come through the Golden Gate from the ocean. She was moving in stately fashion — her silhouette suggesting she was a fast-moving clipper ship — coming into San Francisco. *Maybe,* I preferred to think, *Mother was on her. Maybe Oats was too.*

Observing the ship, Sam said, "Someone took a chance." It was hard to say if he was admiring or criticizing.

"If someone's coming in, someone could go out," I said. "Is the *Yankee Sword* moving?"

Thad put the telescope to his eye. After some fretful waiting on my part, he said, "Not an inch."

Sam said, "I promise: a ship like that won't work against the fog. Not tonight."

Thad handed me the telescope.

I took it and aimed for the points of light. After a while, I could see the ship's profile. Then, as I looked, I saw a few lights moving about on what I took to be her main deck.

"Something's happening on her," I said, and passed the telescope to Sam.

He studied her. "They're lowering jolly boats," he said. "With men in them."

Alarmed, I said, "Think they're coming after us?" I even put a hand to my money belt.

Sam said, "My guess is that since the ship isn't going anywhere, they're allowing crew to go ashore for a last night. That's good. Means they won't come back till morning."

Thad took the telescope and looked. After a while, he said, "Ayuh. That's what they're doing."

It was left to me to say, "Then there will be less of a crew on her."

Sam said, "Right. Not many going to give up last shore night. They'll have only left a short watch."

"How many is short?"

"One. Two."

I said, "Doesn't that make it easier for us to get on her?"

"Could," said Sam. "Unless it's a trick."

"What kind of trick?"

"Pretending not to have a lot of men on board. We have to keep studying her. Need to be patient."

We continued sitting, waiting, and watching.

I did not say anything, nor did the boys. I suspect we all knew what was going to happen: at some point, we were going to board the *Yankee Sword*.

38

T HE CONSTANT, STEADY LAPPING OF LAZY LITTLE
waves against the island shore measured our time. Cold, I
wrapped my braid around my neck like a scarf and hugged my
body while resting my chin on my drawn-up knees. My hair
felt heavy and dirty. My scalp itched. I was also starving, but I
wasn't going to say anything about that. I'm sure the boys were
just as uncomfortable. No one spoke a complaint.

Sitting there, once again I could almost hear Father saying to me, "Try and act a little ladylike." What would Mother
think if she could see me? I even thought about Aunt Lavinia.
What would *she* say if she knew what I was about? She'd have
an eruption. The thought made me smile. But then, with a
plunging heart, I knew that if we didn't rescue Jacob, I must be
the one to tell them. It would be ghastly.

From time to time, we passed the telescope between us, studying the *Yankee Sword*, but saw nothing of note. I was certain that those boats—with the crew—that had left the *Yankee Sword* and headed for the city had not returned. There could be, however, no doubt: at some point, they would return.

I suspect I briefly—once or twice—nodded into sleep. I jerked awake. The lights on the *Yankee Sword* looked to be brighter. I asked myself: Was it because my eyes were fixed upon them so steadily? Or was the fog beginning to thin?

I decided it *was* thinning. We must move. I grew excited even as I felt hollow in my stomach. When the fog fully went, so too would the *Yankee Sword*. Once again, that old urgency: a need to *do* something. Trying to keep my voice steady, I said, "What time do you think it is?"

"Two, three," said Sam.

I stood up and looked around toward the Gate. The fog seemed to have melted away. "The fog's gone," I announced.

The boys stood and looked for themselves.

After a moment, Sam said, "Means, soon as there's some daylight, that crew will come back."

"Which also means," I added, "the *Yankee Sword* will go."

"Likely," said Thad.

Sam said, "As I see it, even if they were worried about us, they wouldn't think we'd go out there. Not now. They might even believe we're still locked up on that rotten ship."

I waited a few moments and then said, "Then we should get on her—now."

"Fine with me," said Sam.

"Ayuh," added Thad.

That was all it took to reach that momentous agreement.

Even so, we continued to stand there, gazing at the *Yankee Sword*. It was as if we needed to measure, not just the distance from where we were to the ship, but our own courage as well.

It was me, at last, who said, "Let's go."

Thad said, "Odds look good."

To which Sam added, "I'm ready."

We lit my lantern but kept the flame small. Moving with care, we climbed down over the island rocks to the water's edge, taking one another's hands when necessary. It was a fact: we three had come to work so well together that there was no need of talk.

It took all of us to get the rowboat off the rocks and back into water. We held the line to keep the bobbing rowboat from floating away. Thad, who had the longest legs, waded out and clambered on. Once set, he pulled the line to get her closer to shore. With a jump from a shoreline rock, Sam boarded her. I was left holding the line. Once he got on, I also leaped aboard, Sam steadying me as I landed.

Thad rowed us to where the *Sadie Rose* was anchored. When he got on, I tied the rowboat to the stern.

As before, Sam was at the ketch's tiller and took command. Under his orders, Thad and I hauled up the mainsail, then the mizzen. Though the wind was light, our sails fluttered and filled. The tiller shifted. The boom swung around and Sam pointed us straight in the direction of the *Yankee Sword*'s lights.

We were on our way.

In the predawn — the darkest time of night — the bay seemed immense, our little vessel small. Waters were calm, broken here and there by flashing flicks of foam. The air was moist, but the fog continued to wane. Like awakening eyes, multiple stars began to appear above. The moon, still woolly, began to brighten and gain an edge, even as feathery clouds streaked across its face. We were about two miles from the city, but I could see some lights. Most important of all, we were drawing ever nearer to the *Yankee Sword*.

As we sailed along, I thought, *Miss Tory, do you understand that you are about to steal upon a ship in the middle of the night? You are like a pirate.* I recalled what Señor Rosales had warned, that what we were doing was peligroso — dangerous. Sí. Muy peligroso.

Would it be wrong to make a confession? At that moment, yes, I was scared, but I was also truly thrilled to be part of this adventure.

Sam had us tacking back and forth across a light, moist headwind, with Thad and me periodically ducking the swinging boom. No one spoke. The only sounds were a slight ruffling of the sails, and the slap of our bow as the *Sadie Rose* spanked through the water, *slap, slip, slap.* The spray of water kept me alert.

Not that I ever took my eyes from the safety lights on the *Yankee Sword.* At first they appeared far away, but as the *Sadie Rose* drew ever nearer, they became bigger, stronger, and brighter. I began to see the outline of the ship, a long, low black shadow against the deeper dark, an island of darksomeness.

From time to time Thad turned and looked toward the city. I looked too. There were only a few lights. Nothing moving.

"What are you looking at?" I asked.

"Want to make sure that crew isn't returning," said Thad.

"You think they will?"

"Absolutely," called Sam from the helm. "By first light." But he didn't look toward the city the way Thad and I did. Perhaps he didn't wish to. I decided he was nervous, the way I was, but I chose not to ask.

I gazed up. The moon kept growing bigger, clearer, even as it lowered in the western sky.

I could see the *Yankee Sword* with increasing clarity: her masts, her spars, her furled sails. Her safety lights never moved. I saw no sign of life on her. I kept wondering how many of the crew had remained on board for the watch. It abruptly occurred to me: if I saw them with any such great clarity, they would see us just as well. Wasn't that what keeping a watch meant?

We drew closer.

Sam sailed the ketch round the *Yankee Sword*'s bow, dodging her anchor line, which was holding the big ship fast. Simultaneously, I reminded myself that we had made no plans for how to board her. Only then did I have yet another thought: *What if Jacob is not on her?*

I whispered, "What do we do now?"

Thad, his voice low, said, "Get on her."

"All of us?"

Sam said, "Someone needs to take care of the ketch. If anyone on the *Yankee Sword* steals her, we'll be dead in the water. And I mean dead."

"I have to go on," I said.

Thad said, "I'll stay. Sam knows ships better than me."

"Can you handle the ketch?" asked Sam.

"Been watching you," said Thad.

"Huh," muttered Sam.

Though I was tense and excited, the boys seemed quite casual. I doubted they felt that way; they must have been masking their worriment.

Sam edged the ketch in until we drew close to the *Yankee*

Sword. Next moment, we jolted softly against her hull, not the city side, I noticed, but the bay side. *Smart.* If the crew returned, we would be less likely to be seen.

All this to say, we had arrived. I don't think my senses had ever been so alert. Now we needed to board her.

39

T HAD STOOD UP IN THE BOW OF THE KETCH, LOW-
lit lantern in hand, in search of lines hanging from the
Yankee Sword. He found them easily enough, most likely the
ones that had been used to let down the crew's boats when
they had gone to the city.

He grabbed two, pulling them hard to make sure they
held. When they did, he passed one to Sam, who tied it to a
cleat on the bow of the *Sadie Rose.* The other line went to our
stern. That kept us stable.

I worked to drop our sails.

We were now held fast to the *Yankee Sword.*

Speaking softly, Sam said, "No talking unless we have
to. Remember: they'll have *someone* on board. Maybe more
than one."

"What about light?" I asked.

"Her safety lights will have to do."

"I'll keep my lantern," said Thad. "That way, you'll know where to come back to."

"If we do," muttered Sam.

"You will," said Thad. Then he added, "Tory, give me your flint in case my lamp goes out."

Briefly, we stood there in our ketch. The *Sadie Rose* rocked, but far less than my beating heart. In the faint yellow light of Thad's little lantern, we looked at one another as if only then fully aware of what we were daring to do. I think only then did I allow myself to acknowledge: *We were going to board her.*

It was Thad who put out a hand. I put a hand on his, and Sam put a hand atop mine. Without words, it was understood: bright hearts in faint light. Oh, how much then did I love my two friends.

"God keep us," Sam whispered.

"Amen," said Thad.

To which I actually said, "Our will is our destiny." Just to say it sent a cold quiver through me.

"I'll go first," said Sam. "It'll be quicker." He reached as high as he could on one of the free lines. Using both hands, he hoisted himself up from the deck of the *Sadie Rose.* Then he began to walk and pull himself aloft. Thad and I, in the ketch, watched him go, his shadow before him. When he reached the topgallant rail, he swung over, and then vanished from sight.

It seemed forever before I saw — if dimly — Sam's head pop up. He didn't call or speak, but made a waving motion. I understood. Things, so far, were safe. It was my turn to climb.

Thad touched me on my back, leaned forward, and whispered into my ear, "Good luck."

Heart hammering, I reached up and grabbed the loose line as high as I could with two hands as I had done before. Then, with all my strength, I hauled myself up from the ketch's deck. As soon as my feet had nothing beneath them, I swung them flat against the *Yankee Sword*'s hull and began to pull and walk.

My efforts were not as hard as the first time I climbed that ship in Rotten Row. Not to say it was easy, but I had a surer sense of what I was doing, and how difficult it was. Which is to say, I knew I could do it. *Had to do it.* Thus, with some swiftness, I moved up, and did not look down, not once.

I grasped the topgallant rail. Sam was waiting. Two hands extended, he helped me up and over. Next moment, I was standing near him on the deck of the *Yankee Sword,* my legs full of trembles, but no more than my heart.

I went back to the rail, looked over and down. Thad was standing on the ketch, peering up. I waved. He waved back. As I watched, he made the flame on his lantern even smaller, in hopes that if anyone was looking out from shore, he would not be seen.

A tap to my shoulder made me swing around to face Sam. He gave me a nod. I understood. We needed to move.

Turning from him, I gazed about the ship. Sam had been right: the glowing lantern hanging from a lower spar cast enough shadowy light to allow us to see most of the main deck. Moonlight helped. There was almost no color, just light and dark. The ship's only movement was a gentle rise and fall.

The deck was cluttered, nothing such as might be called shipshape. But among the vessel's usual paraphernalia—lines, standing blocks, deadeyes, and the like, all of which lay disordered about the deck—we saw no one. Nor did there at first appear to be any place in which someone might hide.

As we stood there, gazing about, there was almost complete silence, a silence broken by the occasional thrum of rigging lines and wires, plus chains and turnbuckles, making fretsome rattles. Bay waters flip-flopped against the ship. The quietude enhanced these meager sounds, and put brittle edges to my nerves, as if they were being plucked.

I reminded myself there had to be *someone* on the ship keeping watch. What's more, the ship's safety lights were meant not only to protect the *Yankee Sword* but also to guide the crew coming back from the city. At some point, they absolutely would come. We needed to hurry.

We had yet to move when Sam noticed the boxlike structure near the stern. He nudged me and pointed. It had a window, and within the box was a feeble light. When I studied it, I could see the top edge of a spoked steering wheel. From where I stood, I could not see anyone.

Sam whispered into my ear, "Steering house. Need to look."

We would have to draw much closer if we were to see if anyone was there.

Walking side by side, we moved toward the stern, working hard to be as quiet as possible.

We soon reached the small structure. Being taller than Sam, I stood on my toes and peeked inside.

What I saw was a man on the floor, sprawled on his back. His eyes were closed. On his rising and falling chest lay a Colt pistol. I could hear his loud snoring and I saw some white spittle on his lips. By the man's feet was a tipped-over whiskey bottle. It appeared empty. To one side stood an oil lantern with a small burning flame, the flame enclosed in a hurricane glass to keep it from blowing out. As far as I could guess, the man was deep in besotted sleep.

But the instant I saw him, I knew who he was: the man with the crooked nose, the one in the police station, the man who had seen me outside the tent, the one I supposed had followed us into Rotten Row and locked Sam and me up. Jacob's jailor. To see him took away any remaining doubts: my brother was on the ship.

I gestured to Sam, wanting him to have a look.

Standing on a deadeye, Sam did, then backed away and gazed at me with great intensity. I mouthed the word "Crimp." He nodded. We both understood: we now knew there was at least one person aboard, and that person was armed. It was obvious: we needed to move faster.

"Where?" I mouthed that word too, rather than saying it.

Sam's reply was a wave of his hand, signaling me to follow. As we went along the deck, he pointed out two companionways fore and aft. Both were open. I looked down into the aft one. There were steps leading down. Below, faint light glowed—a lit lantern, I supposed—which allowed me to see decking beneath the last step. The tween deck.

Sam pointed. He was going below. When he did, I trailed after, descending into the heart of the ship.

We reached the bottom step. Hanging from the timbered ceiling was an oil lamp, which swung with the ship's slight rising and falling motion, as if to suggest that time was moving quickly. Timbers creaked. The lamp's flame was small but shed enough light for me to see the bulky trunks of two masts that rose up from below and on up through the ceiling. Between these fore and mainmasts was a double row of open sleeping berths. From where we stood, it took no more than a glance to see that they were empty. There were also long tables and benches.

Most of the deck space, however, was taken up—along the port and starboard sides—by something like forty doors, all of which were closed. Sam came up to me, leaned close to my ear, pointed to the doors, and whispered, "Staterooms."

I understood. If Jacob was being held on board, more than likely he would be in one of these rooms.

·40·

SAM WENT TO THE STARBOARD DOORS. I WENT TO the port-side ones. Each door had an iron door handle and an empty keyhole. Taking hold of one handle, I pulled. The door opened with ease.

In such faint light as there was, I could see at once that no one was in the room. But there were two beds, one to either side. Also, a small table and chair. On the table, another empty whiskey bottle. A glass. The ship's movement made it roll back and forth. One of the beds had rumpled blankets, suggesting that someone had slept there recently. Had Jacob been there? The whiskey bottle told me otherwise.

I moved to the next door, opened it, and found the same emptiness, but with no evidence that anyone had been there.

I went on to four more staterooms. All were the same, uninhabited. I glanced across the way. Sam was opening and shutting doors. He shook his head. His staterooms were just as bare.

The sixth door I tried to open refused to budge. I yanked harder. It stayed shut.

"Sam," I hissed.

He hurried to my side. I gave another pull with no results. Sam understood. The two of us now gripped the iron doorknob with four hands and yanked, once, twice, with all our strength.

With an ear-splintering *screech*, the door ripped out, bringing part of the frame with it. I peered in. Sitting up in one of the beds, a look of amazement on his dirty face, was my brother Jacob.

I tell you true, my first thought was: *He looks so young.*

"Tory!" he cried, jumping up. His face was pale, his clothing rumpled and torn. No shoes were on his feet. But the joy and relief on his face when he realized it was me was everything I could have wished.

When I rushed forward and threw my arms about him, he burst into tears, but all the same managed to say, "I never thought you'd come."

"Of course I would," I returned like a proper book heroine. "This is Sam, my friend. We'll talk later. We need to move fast. Keep quiet. Come on."

From then on, all our efforts were bent on getting free of the ship.

"Follow me," whispered Sam, leading the way. Then came Jacob. Then I. Once out of the stateroom, we hurried toward the companionway steps, the same upon which we'd come down. Sam went up the first few risers, turned, and held out his hand. Jacob took it. They started up.

That's when we heard, from directly overhead, steps moving about on the main deck—heavy, irregular steps, as if the one walking were unsure of his direction.

Sam pointed up and, speaking softly, said, "That man we saw. He's about."

I understood: it was the man in the wheelhouse cabin, the one who had been in a drunken stupor, the one with the Colt pistol on his chest. The loud noise we'd made when ripping open the door to the room in which Jacob was being held must have woken him.

Sam made a motion which told Jacob to back down the steps. He did so quickly. I too retreated. Then the three of us stood in the dim light, looking up, straining to listen, not daring to move or make any sound.

A garbled shout came from above: "Some . . . body here? I heard you. Who the devil . . . are you?"

I made a quick decision. Whispering to Sam, I said, "Stay with Jacob. I'll use the forward companionway, go up, and try to get the man's attention. Lead him away. When I do, bring Jacob up to the deck. Get him to Thad."

"But—"

"Do it," I said, without thinking how abrupt I must have sounded. My sole excuse is that I was *not* going to be thwarted in my rescue of Jacob. And if anyone should take the greater risk, it must be I.

Leaving Sam and Jacob, I raced along the tween deck until I came to the forward steps. Once there, I dashed up as fast as I could and stepped out on deck. As soon as I did, I spun about and looked toward the stern.

By the light of the lower spar lantern, I saw the broken-nosed man standing there, the one we'd seen in the wheelhouse. Clearly having trouble standing upright, he was stumbling about, showing every evidence of being thoroughly drunk. Even so, in one hand he was gripping his Colt pistol, waving it in the air. In his other hand was the lit oil lantern. He was holding it over the companionway, trying to see below.

"Who's there?" he cried. "Come on up . . . do you hear?" He pointed his wavering pistol down.

"I'm right here," I shouted from behind him.

With a heavy lurch, the man managed to swing about and drop into a stooping posture. From under his beetled brows, he stared in my direction, eyes squinted, suggesting his vision was none too clear.

"Were you calling me?" I shouted.

Swaying from side to side, head thrust forward, the man stayed in place. I was certain he was trying to make sense of what he was seeing and hearing, which is to say, me.

"Come over here . . . you," he yelled, making a summoning gesture with the pistol. His speech was all slithered.

"If you're trying to get me," I returned, "you'll have to come where I am."

He seemed to be struggling to see me, because his body continued to waver and his head—birdlike—moved side to side, as if he were adjusting his sight. He also held his lantern higher to see me better. "Who . . . the devil are you?" he cried out. "What are you doing here?"

He did not appear to recognize me.

"Come closer," I said. "I'll answer you."

"You've no b . . . bloody business being here," the man bellowed, extending the arm with the pistol in my direction. "I can shoot you," he proclaimed. "I will. And . . . I can." He had yet to move from where he was.

Trying to coax him nearer, I stepped backward, moving in the direction of the ship's bow, though never taking my eyes from him. But one time when I moved, he lifted his pistol and fired straight up into the air. The explosion was thunderous, made me cower, and set my heart to pounding. It took the greatest effort to remain in place and not flee.

The man began to advance upon me, his lantern swinging wildly even as his body staggered side to side. Since he kept his pistol pointed—more or less—in my direction, I was all too aware that he could pull the trigger at any moment. Wanting—needing—to lure him farther toward me, I continued to back up, keeping an eye underfoot so as not to trip over something on the cluttered deck. It worked. As I retreated, the broken-nosed man moved in equal measure with numb-footed steps.

That was when I saw, out of the corner of my eye, just what I was hoping for. Sam, now a good way behind the man on the deck, emerged cautiously from the aft companionway. What's more, I could see Jacob on Sam's back, clinging to his neck. Dim though the light was, I could see my brother's frightened eyes staring at the drunken man. The man with the pistol was so intent on me, he never looked behind.

"I'll kill you," the man shouted to me, waving his pistol while taking more clumsy steps in my direction. "I will," he shouted.

I edged backward, only to have the man come forward that much more.

Sam rose fully up from below.

Once he was free of the steps and fully on the deck, he moved with silent speed to the port side of the ship. I don't know how or where he found the strength, but he climbed atop the rail with Jacob still holding on. Then Sam grabbed a spar line and hoisted himself up, Jacob with him. Next moment, Sam—with Jacob clinging to him—swung out and away from the ship, dropped, and disappeared. At the same moment, I heard Sam shout, "Thad!"

I heard a splash.

My thought: *Was Thad there?*

The man who was stalking me also must have heard. He spun about and looked to see who had made the call and splash. He was too late: Sam and Jacob were not there.

All I wanted to do was to see where Sam and Jacob had gone—if they were safe—but the man who was stalking me now whirled about, extended his wavering arm and pistol in my direction, and pulled the trigger.

The explosion was deafening. I ducked, but I need not have done so. His aim was so undirected, I have no idea where the bullet went, or even if it was close to me.

Seeing he hadn't struck me, the man, now furious, charged forward, as though intent on striking me bodily with his pistol. That was when his foot became entangled with something on the deck. Doddering to begin with, he now tumbled forward and fell. As he fell, he extended his hands forward. They struck the deck. That caused the pistol to fire off another shot. Another wild miss. But also, the lantern he'd been holding in his hand struck and shattered, spewing oil all about.

In an instant, a flash of flame shot up, a brilliant orange-red geyser, two, three feet high. Wherever the oil spilled, fire began to spread with violent speed.

Despite his stupefaction, the man grasped what was happening: the blaze was spreading. Panicky, he pulled himself up to his knees, dropped his pistol, and began to swat at the flames with both his bare hands.

It was to no avail. The inferno grew, disgorging black plumes of smoke that became part of the night. The look on the man's face—made scarlet with the light of the fire—was full of dread.

I didn't stop to see what else the man did. Realizing that he was no longer watching me, that his gun was out of his hand, I raced to the topgallant rail and scrambled up, my terror no doubt giving me extra strength. In seconds I was standing atop the rail, waving my arms for balance.

I glanced back: the fierce fire was spreading, mounting.

"Thad!" I shouted, and without looking, I jumped off the ship into nothing, even as I had the thought: *I can't swim.*

·41·

HOW LONG DID IT TAKE ME TO REACH THE WATER? It *seemed* forever. It also felt no more than half a second. If that is a contradiction, so be it. All I know is that I hit the cold water hard, painfully so, and instantly began to sink.

Sputtering, struggling for breath, my arms wild in their motion, I somehow rose up to the surface. I struggled, flailed, sank. But then I was grabbed by hands, followed by a grip around my shoulders, which pulled me up.

It was Thad—in the water at my side—who held me. Such was my trust, I stopped struggling. For some moments, we floundered, but he supported me.

The next thing I realized was that the *Sadie Rose* had come up, and many hands, Sam's, Jacob's, and Thad's, were dragging and shoving me onto the deck of the ketch.

I lay on our little ship, spewing and dripping water, gagging, while Jacob thumped me on my back, far too much. I was soaking wet, cold, and no doubt trembling too. I was aware our little ship was drifting. But mostly, I knew I was alive and my dear Jacob was next to me. As I lay there, I managed to say, "Are you all right?"

"Uh-huh," he said, but his eyes—I realized—were not on me but on something else. Puzzled, I shifted and pulled myself around so as to see at what he was staring.

I could hardly believe what I saw.

Not so very far from us, the *Yankee Sword* was engulfed in fire.

It was as if I were seeing a gigantic red rose, a rose twisting and turning in agony, as petal-like flames spurted in all directions, creating a radiance that pressed and poked into the darkness of the waning night. Masts and spars were fingers of fire, illuminating rising clouds of scarlet smoke. The air was thick with the smell of burning wood, tar, and canvas, the heat of the fire—even at a distance—hot upon my face. All I could hear was a crackling and hissing, the sound of the ship being consumed. In truth, the *Yankee Sword*'s hull, long, low, and black, lay altogether motionless, lifeless midst the frenzied fire.

It was Sam who cried out, "They're coming back."

"What?"

"The *Yankee Sword* crew."

The light of the burning *Yankee Sword*, helped by the growing dawn, enabled me to see two jolly boats coming from the direction of the city. They were full of men—perhaps as many as four to a side—straining at multiple oars, moving rapidly toward the *Yankee Sword*. But as I watched, one of the jolly boats began to slow down. It was as if only then did the crew realize that their ship was doomed. Then one of the boats, as if under command, *turned* toward the *Sadie Rose*. We had been too intent upon the burning ship. It took but a moment for us to realize they were racing toward *us*.

Thad leaped to haul up the sail. Sam tore aft to grab the tiller. I was still too dazed and out of breath to lend a hand. Jacob, in his own state of panic, was of no use whatsoever.

The boom swept over my head. Our ketch heeled. We tacked *away* from those rowboats. I knew we were now moving, but I also realized we were not going fast.

The jolly boat, however, was, without doubt, coming right toward us with great swiftness, her multiple oars working in unison, propelling her forward at great speed so that white foam curled before her sharp prow as before a high-nosed shark.

I also saw that a man was standing in the bow of that boat. The light of the fire allowed me see his white head of hair, his beard. I recognized him: Captain Littlefield of the *Yankee Sword*. He must have seen the *Sadie Rose* when we were sailing about the bay. Connecting us to the fire, he was now coming after us.

As streaks of morning sunlight began to strengthen in the eastern sky, Sam tried to sail us away from Littlefield, toward the protection of the city. But we were moving much too slowly, whether because of adverse currents or little wind, I cannot say.

Littlefield's jolly boat was not impeded by such restraints. On the contrary: her multiple oars meant she was quickly gaining on us.

"You need to go faster," I shouted.

"Can't," returned Sam, whose constant looking back told me he was well aware of—and alarmed by—what was happening.

I glanced toward the *Yankee Sword.* The fires on her had much subsided when I heard a great *hissing* sound. By the dawn's light, I watched as plumes of black smoke turned white, the white of steam. Flames suddenly shrank. Next moment, those same flames vanished, and nothing was left upon the bay waters save smoke, which hovered over the bay like a slowly fading spirit.

"She's sunk," said Thad in an awe-filled voice.

"Glory be," muttered Sam.

"Stop!" ordered a voice over the water.

I spun about and realized that while we had been staring

at the sinking *Yankee Sword,* Littlefield and his jolly boat had drawn that much closer, gaining on us every moment. The captain, like a whaleboat harpooner, stood in the bow.

"He's going to ram us," I cried.

Thad leaped up and looked back with a fierceness I had never seen on him before. In his hand was a mallet, which had been left on the ketch. For his part, Sam had found a belaying pin and was clutching that even as he clung to the tiller. As for me, I pulled the knife from my money belt, though what I — or we — intended to use such for, I cannot say I had any idea. The notion that we, with our makeshift weapons, could repel them was absurd.

Sam dropped down and tried to maneuver the ketch away from the rowboat, only to shift us directly into headwinds, which is to say, our boat simply ceased to move. In irons, as sailors say — dead in the water.

As for Littlefield's jolly boat, the multiple oars were moving her ever faster, quickly gaining on us. As she drew closer, I saw Captain Littlefield bend down and then stand. Something was in his hands. It was an anchor attached to a line. He was holding the anchor by its shaft.

When his jolly boat was within ten feet of us, he heaved the anchor at us. Perfectly thrown, one of the anchor flukes neatly hooked our gunwale so that we were tied to him. Then Littlefield began to draw in the taut line — and us — while the rowers kept up their rowing, and since we were being held right in their furious path, we must be crushed.

That was when I leaped forward and, with my knife, desperately sawed through the taut anchor line. Like an opening fist, fingers of cordage sprang apart. The line was severed.

As though released from a grip, our ketch sprung free.

On the instant, Sam shifted the tiller hard, thereby catching a wind. The boom swung over our heads like a scythe. We heeled over at such a deep angle, bay water began to trickle into the boat. It seemed we were about to be swamped; my heart misgave. Next second, Sam turned us again, righted the ketch, and headed out into the open bay. The scuppers let the water flow out. Thad found a bucket from somewhere and began to bail as well. Jacob and I, making cups of our hands, worked too. The more water we dumped, the faster we moved.

I looked back. Captain Littlefield and his boat were being left far behind.

"Look," I said. "They've stopped coming."

Thad stood up. "We're away!" he cheered.

"Hurrah!" cried Jacob.

It was only then that Thad looked down at me and said, "Good thing you had that knife."

"Thank Father," I replied, and gave Jacob a squeeze.

Sam steered the *Sadie Rose* farther out, putting more and more distance between us and Littlefield and his crew.

By then we were all grinning fools.

Then, feeling secure and out of reach, Sam made a big loop and, by the light of a blooming dawn, came around into Yerba Buena Cove.

It was not long before the *Sadie Rose*—in full dawn—was threading her way among the ships of Rotten Row. They were so large, and our ketch so small, I had no doubt we were well hidden. What had once been only hundreds of ugly, decaying vessels, ships that had repulsed and frightened me, now became our protection, our fortress, and our walls of defense.

Rotten Row had become our place of safety.

·42·

HOW HE DID IT, I DON'T KNOW, BUT SAM maneuvered the *Sadie Rose* to the approximate place where we had begun. Once there, I heaved our anchor out into the shallow water. Thad dropped the ketch sails, then hauled in the rowboat. I got into the stern seat and placed Jacob next to me, my arm tightly around him. Sam got in. Finally, Thad. Settled, we shoved away from the *Sadie Rose,* her FOR SALE and FREE signs still attached. I was happy to leave her behind.

"Not sure we should go to the cove beach," said Sam. "Be safer for us to head for Happy Valley. If we need to, we can hide in my tent."

Nobody objected, and Thad and Sam rowed side by side, pulling hard. From time to time I'd look back. No one was coming after us.

It was only as we went along that Jacob told us what had happened to him.

It was the night that Thad and I returned so late from fishing down-bay. Exceedingly worried as to where I might be, Jacob searched all over for us, and at one point—knowing how Thad liked to gamble—went into the crowded Mercury. That was when he was approached by a man—his description fit Mr. Kassel. Kassel asked what Jacob was doing there. When Jacob told him whom he was looking for, the man offered help in finding me. He also gave Jacob some gingerbread and lemonade, which a hungry Jacob took and consumed. The lemonade must have been drugged, because the next thing Jacob knew, he was locked up on a ship.

He was on one such ship and then another, before being taken to the *Yankee Sword*. His jailor was the man with the broken nose. I never did learn his name. No more than I knew his fate.

But Jacob's tale was much as Sam had told me it might have happened. While we had a successful rescue, we also knew how close we'd come to something otherwise. It kept us quiet. The boys rowed. I stayed close to Jacob. When we came ashore and stepped out on land, Happy Valley was a happy place for me.

Sam led the way in the dawn light to his tent where his father, Mr. Nichols, greeted us with a mixture of warmth and alarm as Sam related all that had happened. Mr. Nichols was simultaneously angry with Sam and proud of him, the way parents will be when their child does something foolish but brave. But after congratulations, warnings were offered. "Mr. Kassel will be looking for you, all of you. You'll need to be careful."

Seeing me shivering with cold and weariness, he said, "You, Miss Tory and Jacob, need to go home. Thad—is that your name?—best go with them. Sam, be so good to show them the way. But—hear me? You come right on back."

"Yes, sir."

So it was that once again Sam led me—plus Jacob and Thad—through and out of Happy Valley. When we reached its edge, I found myself suddenly reluctant to part from him. I gave him a hug—as did Jacob—which he returned. He and Thad shook hands as if grown men. I had to smile. They were still boys to me.

"Can't you hug each other?" I cried. Grinning sheepishly, they did.

"Let's meet soon," I said.

That being affirmed, and knowing we were not truly parting, allowed us to go our ways.

Thad, Jacob, and I worked through the city up to our tent, keeping a watch about us as we went. Exhausted, by the time we got home, our steps were slow. Even as we came up to the tent by morning's light, Señor Rosales spied us coming and ran out to meet us. "¡Corderita! Jacob! Welcome home. Tell me what's happened."

We told him the tale as much as we could.

"You'll need to find a place to hide," he said. "That man with the broken nose—if he survived—he knows where you live, doesn't he? And when was the last time you ate?"

When I told him, he said, "I'll bring some food. Then, I'll keep a lookout from my café."

You may be sure I thanked him profusely.

Thad stood there awkwardly. "I better be going," he said.

Jacob, all his dislike gone, gave him an embrace; then, as if embarrassed, ran into the tent.

"Thank you," I said to Thad, and impulsively gave him another hug, which he returned awkwardly.

"We did some fine good," he called as he headed up the hill.

By the time I got into the tent, Jacob was already on his bed, blanket up to his chin, happy to be home. Within moments, Señor Rosales brought us beefsteaks and coffee. Jacob and I devoured it all.

"Tory," said Jacob when we were finally alone, "I didn't know if I'd ever see you again."

"The same," I returned. Then I added, "I hope you heard what Sam's father said: we're going to have to be careful. Keep looking about."

"Do we have to hide somewhere?"

"I can't believe that man survived. He was terribly drunk. He's the only one who knows where we live."

For a moment, we just lay on our beds, appreciating the silent calm.

"Tory?"

"What?"

"Think Father and Mother will be coming soon?" This time he asked it reluctantly, as if afraid of the answer.

"It's December," I said. "They should be here soon. Father promised. Mother? I don't know. Any day, hopefully."

Within moments, I heard Jacob's soft, breathy sleep.

For a while, I lay there, running through all that had happened. In doing so, I renewed my gratitude for what Thad and Sam had done. How could I ever return such favors, particularly to Sam? I also allowed myself to feel pride for what I'd accomplished. How much I had changed since Providence days.

That led to Jacob's question coming into my head: *Where are Father and Mother? What if they don't come?*

I quickly scolded myself. *They will come.*

But then—how could it be otherwise?—another question came: *When they do come, what will they say—and do—about all that I have become?*

·43·

MORNING CAME, AND JACOB SLEPT LATER THAN I. As I lay abed, waiting for him to wake, my hunger was such that I went across the way, where Señor Rosales was already at work, feeding a line of men.

"¡Corderita!" he called out when he saw me. "¿Cómo estás? Sleep well?"

"I'll be fine," I assured him.

He beckoned me close, then leaned forward and whispered, "You need to know, the whole morning the talk here is about the burning of the *Yankee Sword*. I said nothing. *Nada.* The rumor is one man died."

"I'll go to the mayor's office. I should tell him what happened."

"Do you wish me to go with you?"

"Gracias, but I think it best if I go alone—with Jacob."

Then he offered me some beef. I wondered if he ever tired of cooking it.

Once Jacob got up and ate some food, the two of us went to Portsmouth Square, where the office of the alcalde—as the city's mayor was called—was. Happily, the only one who was there was Mr. John Geary, the mayor himself. I had seen him about town, for he was hard to miss. A huge man, he was more than six feet tall, quite heavy, and always well dressed.

He seemed puzzled by my showing up—with Jacob— and asked, in a friendly fashion, what I wished.

"Please, sir, I need to tell you what happened to the *Yankee Sword.*"

"Can you?" he returned, clearly surprised, but immediately interested.

I told him our story, with me doing most of the talking, though Jacob added his tale of how he had been crimped.

Mr. Geary listened to us and spoke little, growing graver as we went on. When we were done, he said, "You've been brave." He did not reveal what he would do, if anything, but he did say, "I think the two of you may consider yourselves safe."

As I would later learn, there were no arrests. But before two days had passed, Thad discovered that Chief Fallon had resigned his position and gone to live far across the bay. Captain Littlefield vanished, presumably sailing away on another ship. As for Mr. Kassel, the *Alta California* reported that he had removed to Sacramento to build himself a new saloon.

Finally, a few days later, when about town, I saw the man with the broken nose. When I spied him, I was taken aback, having assumed that he had perished. That said, his hands were bandaged and he had bruises on his face. Captain Littlefield must have pulled him from the water.

As for me, dressed as I was at the moment, in my feminine attire, he did not recognize me. Then again, acting like a lady is the best disguise.

Even so, I was much alarmed and felt fear that he was back in the city. Might he not seek revenge upon me? Then I realized that he had a sea chest on his shoulder and was going downhill. Feeling the need to see where he was heading—so I could avoid the area—I followed him at a careful distance. To my great relief, he went down to the cove, and I watched as he climbed into a lighter and was carried out to a ship that I knew voyaged to the Sandwich Islands. I even saw him board the vessel, thus gaining the satisfaction and relief of knowing he was going far away. Indeed, I never saw him again.

So much for my enemies.

When Jacob and I left the alcalde's office, my brother asked if we could go to the post office and see if there was any mail from Mother or Father. Once there, we stood in the long line for perhaps an hour, during which time I reminded Jacob that he must not be disappointed if no letter was there for us. But to our amazement, there *was* a letter, one addressed to Mr. Randolph Blaisdell. The moment it was handed out to us, I recognized Mother's handwriting.

We had taken no more than two steps away from the building when I tore the letter open.

"What does she say?" cried Jacob, fairly well dancing about me.

I spoke even as I scanned the letter. "She wrote it months ago but says she is planning to leave Rhode Island in three weeks' time. By clipper ship."

"But when will she arrive?"

I tried to calculate. "If all goes well," I said, trying to sound optimistic, "very soon."

As we walked back to the tent, Jacob was excited. "Then Father will come," he said. "I know he will. And we'll all be together again."

He babbled on about all the things he would tell them, resolving to stand watch every day at the cove beach for their arrival so he could lead them to our tent.

Was I glad? Of course. But I could not refrain from asking the question I had asked myself the night before: *What will Mother say—and do—about all that I have become?* So that I too kept thinking, *I hope they come soon.* But a tiny voice—to my shame and guilt—whispered, *What will I do if they insist I return to what I was?*

During the next few days, Jacob's and my life resumed what it had been. I worked, helping Mr. Lyall with his carpentry on the house he was building. Jacob, as he had promised, spent his time at the cove beach watching for Mother and Father as ships came in. He made sure to come by often to where I was working, to assure me he was safe.

I saw Thad, who resumed his work at the Howard & Mellus store. In turn, he told me Sam had come around to tell him that he and his father were now playing at the El Dorado saloon.

"Is it good for them?"

"Don't think it pays much."

With much back and forth amongst us, we agreed to meet the following Sunday at noon on Goat Hill.

So it was that the three of us, Thad, Sam, and I, sat upon the summit of Goat Hill. (Jacob stayed with Señor Rosales.) I brought along one of the señor's beefsteaks and my knife. Thad brought bread. Sam brought a jug of good water and his bugle.

It was a bright, clear day. As we ate, we gazed at Alcatraces Island while watching new ships arriving in the cove. I told them that my mother might well be on one of them.

"Maybe on the same ship as my mother and sister," said Thad.

Sam told us about his mother and two sisters — about whom we had not heard before. "They'll be waiting for us to come back. Been a year now."

I admitted I wanted both my parents to arrive but was much worried as to what they would say about how I was living.

"What might they do?" asked Sam.

"Not sure," I said. "Back in Providence, I wouldn't have been even allowed to be here, with you."

"Ayuh," said Thad.

"Think your father will have a lot of gold?" asked Sam.

"Doubt it. What's playing at the El Dorado like?"

"Bigger than the Mercury, but they don't listen any better there."

"Do you make more money?" Thad asked.

"Nope. But my father says, if we can keep saving some — a little at a time — we might have enough money to pay passage home in about a year."

"How much do you need?"

"Five hundred."

"If I make that at the tables," Thad promised as he had before, "you can have it."

"But you rarely win," said Sam, laughing.

In truth, most of our talk was to go over all that had happened with us when we rescued Jacob — from when I met Sam at the Mercury to stepping ashore at Happy Valley. It was clear: we truly regretted that the adventure was over and wished we did not have to return to our lives as they were. In fact, we debated about sailing away on the ketch, disputing amongst ourselves with laughing arguments as to where we might best sail: New York, said Sam; over to the gold diggings, urged Thad; while I suggested the most exotic, China.

At some point, Sam picked up his key bugle and played "I Often Think of Writing Home."

I will admit, I shed some tears. The boys did not tease. And why should they? Their eyes were also bright.

Late afternoon, we headed back down, then each of us to our ways, Sam to the El Dorado, Thad to his Howard & Mellus job, me to my tent. When I approached, I saw Jacob sitting outside. Soon as I appeared, he jumped up and ran toward me. He was grinning broadly.

"Guess who's here?"

"Who?"

"Mother!"

It was indeed she, having landed that afternoon after a five months' voyage by way of clipper ship. Jacob — to his vast delight — had seen her come ashore and with great excitement guided her to our tent.

Her astonishment (and incomprehension) as to what she saw of San Francisco was hardly different from our own when we had arrived. As for our residing in a tent, that seemed beyond her understanding. She seemed, in fact, quite dazed. We struggled to answer her endless questions, and it was a measure as to how much Jacob and I had changed that we could actually offer so many explanations suggesting it was all ordinary.

When we had first come to San Francisco, it was as if we had come to a foreign land. Now it was Mother who felt like a foreigner and had to be instructed in how we lived. It was as if we had become her parents.

But of course, Mother's biggest question, *Where is Father?*, had no answer. "Why did he leave you alone? How could he ask you to live here? Has he sent no news? Has he found gold? What do you do for money? What do you eat? Tory, why are you dressed so outlandishly? Where are your ladylike clothes? But what kind of work do you do? Jacob, why aren't you going to school?"

As far as I was concerned, these were all *Providence* questions. We gave San Francisco answers. And when we told Mother about all that had happened to Jacob and how he was rescued, she was nothing less than astonished.

I shall say this: it is a fine thing to have your mother look upon you with amazement and, yes, pride.

As the days passed, Mother struggled to cope, and I had to deal with one constant question: "Tory, must you do things this way?"

That said, she could not argue with the obvious: I was taking care of everything. And, let it be said, she was *not* Aunt Lavinia. She did not order or dictate. Still, she constantly urged with the refrain, "You will really need to change when Father returns with his gold."

I tried to explain that when Father returned, he might — like so many others — not have much gold, but Mother simply could not believe in that possibility.

As for Señor Rosales, Mother, after some hesitation, became his friend. Anyone who had helped her children *had* to be a friend. Besides, Jacob and I now called him Tío Rosales, which is to say, *Uncle* Rosales. A vast improvement on our aunt. He had become our family.

Two weeks passed. During that time I continued to work, and when I could, sneaked away to visit with Thad and Sam. Each of us, in our way, was dissatisfied with what we were doing. Thad was bored with his job. Sam was all too aware how long it would be before he and his father could go back east. As for my mother and I, it was a tug-of-war. I could only hope that when Father returned, his gold searching would have changed him.

Then he did return.

·44·

IT WAS THE WEEK BEFORE CHRISTMAS. MOTHER, Jacob, and I were sitting in the tent, eating the dinner I had cooked. Utterly unexpected, Father simply pulled aside the front flap and there he was. Needless to say, we were as astonished as we were overjoyed, though he was filthy, sick, and exhausted. We truly dragged him inside, set him down, and peppered him with questions.

The tale he told was woeful; his search for gold had been painful, and most melancholy. Backbreaking labor. Cold. Wet. Difficulties with other miners. Overall, he had found no more than three hundred dollars' worth of gold.

None of this mattered—at first. We made him eat, rest, and insisted that he not worry. Mother and I assured him that I, with my work, was bringing in enough funds to keep us going. Having little choice, we stayed where we were, in the tent. Father rested and gradually recovered his strength.

Our Christmas was us and Tío Rosales, which is to say our whole family.

Only after some time had passed did I tell Father what had happened to us, to Jacob. He shook his head and said, "I am sorry."

To which I said, "You need not be. I was able to do everything."

To my great satisfaction, he said, "You did."

Afterward, Mother and I had many a private conversation, trying to decide what our family should do. We considered many things, from returning to Rhode Island to all of us going up-bay to the diggings and searching for gold. We could come to no satisfactory conclusion. In any case, I absolutely refused to go back east.

After a month had gone by, it was clear that Father, now mostly recovered, had absolutely no desire to return to the diggings. His gold fever had broken. He decided to seek employment in the city.

We managed to purchase (at exorbitant prices) new clothing for him and made sure he was clean and shaved. The result: although he was thinner, he was much improved in health and appearance. It worked. To his and our great joy, he found employment with Mr. Thomas Wells, the city's most important banker.

How quickly then our lives changed. A house — to be sure, smaller, less comfortable, than our Providence home — was found. Built by Mr. Lyall (and me!), Mother took it over and made it as comfortable as possible.

The Baptist school opened, and Jacob began to go to school and was much happier, indeed content.

I had never seen my family — Jacob, Father, and Mother — so happy. It was almost exactly what Father had wished for in Providence: "The only thing that will change is our geography." And I knew Aunt Lavinia was a part of our past.

But what of me? I *had* changed: I had become completely independent. At least I thought so; my parents did not.

Jacob didn't care what I did with my days, but my parents surely did. While they were content to reclaim their lives much as they had lived them before in Rhode Island, they wished me to do the same.

I would not.

My parents were not pleased that I kept on working, and that when I worked, I dressed in such fashion that allowed me to labor. Nor did they like it that after I had taken care of them and Jacob, I came and went as I pleased, or that Sam and Thad continued to be my friends.

The three of us met as often as we could. To be sure, we still talked about Jacob's rescue, but over time, less and less. Rather, we talked about what we would like to do.

Sam, as ever, wanted to return to his home.

Thad began to say he wanted to try his hand in the gold fields.

I said I just wished to live without constant remarks about how I should act.

It was Thad who put all these ideas together and made the suggestion: "I think we should go to the diggings and get enough gold so Sam here and his father can get back to their home."

"Think we could?" said Sam.

"Ayuh."

"And how do you suppose we could even get to the gold fields?" I said.

"The ketch," said Thad.

For a moment, no one said anything. Then I said, "Is she still out there?"

"I saw her two days ago."

"Truly?"

Thad grinned. "Got on her. She's just as we left her."

I looked to Sam.

"I don't know," he said. "Sure, my dad would love the

money to go, but not me heading out there to get it. The two of us had a bad time before. But . . ." He turned to me. "You for it?"

"I don't think my parents would like it either."

"Which means?" said Thad.

"I have to think about it."

I did not speak the entire truth. I knew exactly what I wished to do. The question was, How was I to tell my parents?

Later, I sat my parents down — Jacob was not there — and began by saying, "Without my friend Sam, Jacob would not be with us."

I related yet again how Sam was the one who told me what had happened to Jacob. I also made sure they understood all he had done to help save him, even losing his job. Then I went on to relate his story, how he and his father had come seeking gold, only to be driven from the diggings. Finally, I told them what happened to Sam's brother.

I said, "I need to find a way to thank him, and the best way is to find enough gold so they can get back to New York State."

Then I added, "I am not asking permission to go. I just want you to know where I'm going with my two best friends."

That is to say, I gave them no choice.

So it was that one week later, Thad, Sam, and I were on

the ketch, sailing eastward into the bay, heading for the gold fields. We had our pans, shovels, and food. Of course, we also changed our little boat's name. She was no longer called the *Sadie Rose*. The name, which I had crudely painted on her stern, was:

Our Destiny

·Author's Note·

What happened to the hundreds of ships that made up Rotten Row? Many rotted away or were stripped of their wood for building in the city. Some were converted to other uses, such as a church, a jail, warehouses, and saloons. But many were deliberately sunk in Yerba Buena Cove and used as landfill, as land was extended from Montgomery Street to what is now the Embarcadero. So it is that when building foundations were (and still are) constructed, the remains of these old ships are often found. A part of one such ship, the *Niantic,* may be seen in San Francisco's Maritime Museum.

Tory's home, 15 Sheldon Street, in Providence, Rhode Island, is a real place and may be seen on Google Maps. A family named Blaisdell lived there until 1848.

The etiquette instructions provided for Tory's dance school come from lesson books of the day.

San Francisco is still an amazing place.

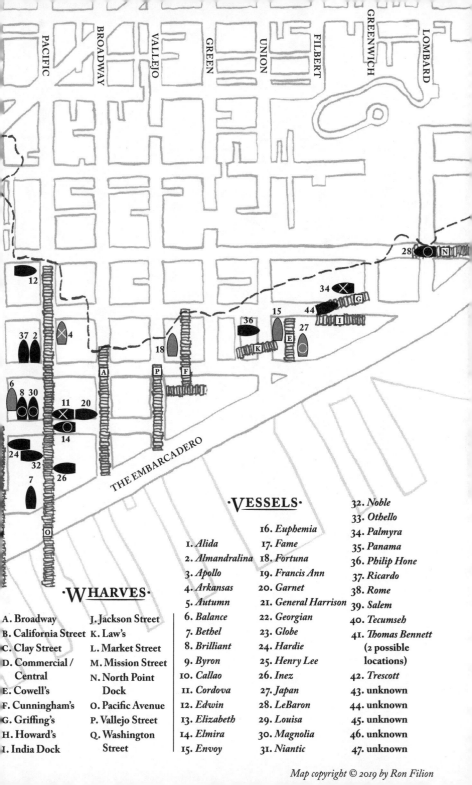

PACIFIC · BROADWAY · VALLEJO · GREEN · UNION · FILBERT · GREENWICH · LOMBARD

THE EMBARCADERO

·WHARVES·

A. Broadway
B. California Street
C. Clay Street
D. Commercial / Central
E. Cowell's
F. Cunningham's
G. Griffing's
H. Howard's
I. India Dock
J. Jackson Street
K. Law's
L. Market Street
M. Mission Street
N. North Point Dock
O. Pacific Avenue
P. Vallejo Street
Q. Washington Street

·VESSELS·

1. *Alida*
2. *Almandralina*
3. *Apollo*
4. *Arkansas*
5. *Autumn*
6. *Balance*
7. *Bethel*
8. *Brilliant*
9. *Byron*
10. *Callao*
11. *Cordova*
12. *Edwin*
13. *Elizabeth*
14. *Elmira*
15. *Envoy*
16. *Euphemia*
17. *Fame*
18. *Fortuna*
19. *Francis Ann*
20. *Garnet*
21. *General Harrison*
22. *Georgian*
23. *Globe*
24. *Hardie*
25. *Henry Lee*
26. *Inez*
27. *Japan*
28. *LeBaron*
29. *Louisa*
30. *Magnolia*
31. *Niantic*
32. *Noble*
33. *Othello*
34. *Palmyra*
35. *Panama*
36. *Philip Hone*
37. *Ricardo*
38. *Rome*
39. *Salem*
40. *Tecumseh*
41. *Thomas Bennett*
   (2 possible locations)
42. *Trescott*
43. unknown
44. unknown
45. unknown
46. unknown
47. unknown

Map copyright © 2019 by Ron Filion